GERALD MESSADIÉ

RAMSÈS II
L'IMMORTEL

☥

LE DIABLE FLAMBOYANT

roman

l'Archipel

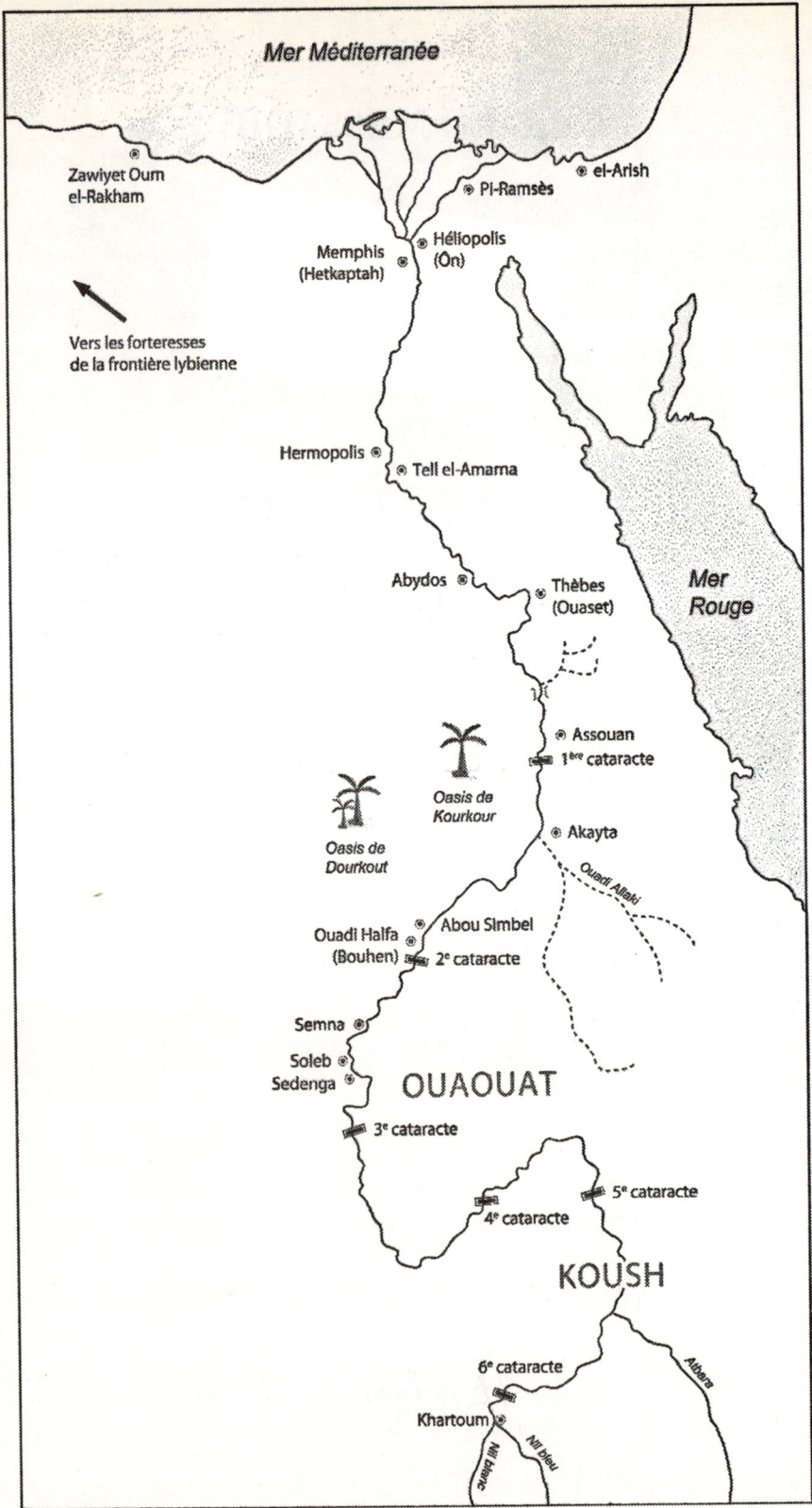

Mer Méditerranée

Zawiyet Oum ⊗
el-Rakham

⊗ el-Arish

⊗ Pi-Ramsès

Memphis ⊗   Héliopolis
(Hetkaptah)   (On)

*Vers les forteresses
de la frontière lybienne*

Hermopolis ⊗

⊗ Tell el-Amarna

Abydos ⊗

Thèbes ⊗
(Ouaset)

**Mer
Rouge**

⊗ Assouan
1ère cataracte

*Oasis de
Kourkour*

⊗ Akayta

Ouadi Allaki

*Oasis de
Dourkout*

Ouadi Halfa ⊗   Abou Simbel
(Bouhen)   2e cataracte

Semna ⊗

Soleb ⊗
Sedenga ⊗

OUAOUAT

3e cataracte

5e cataracte

4e cataracte

KOUSH

6e cataracte

Atbara

Khartoum ⊗

Nil blanc   *Nil bleu*

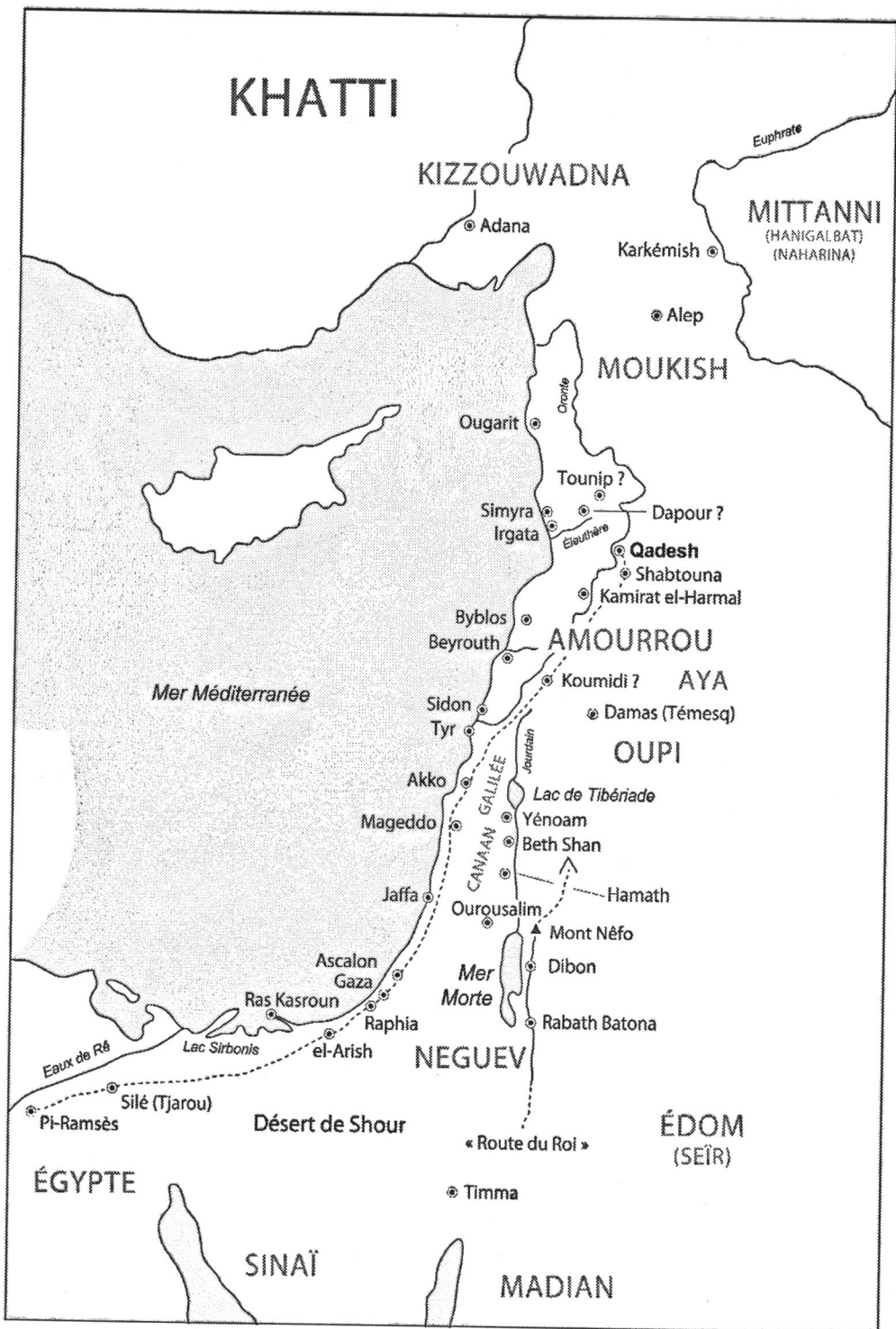

KHATTI

KIZZOUWADNA

⊙ Adana

Karkémish ⊙

MITTANNI
(HANIGALBAT)
(NAHARINA)

⊙ Alep

MOUKISH

⊙ Ougarit

Oronte

Tounip ? ⊙

Simyra ⊙
Irgata ⊙ — Dapour ?

Eleuthère

⊙ **Qadesh**
⊙ Shabtouna
⊙ Kamirat el-Harmal

Byblos ⊙
Beyrouth ⊙

AMOURROU

⊙ Koumidi ?   AYA

Mer Méditerranée

Sidon ⊙
Tyr ⊙

⊙ Damas (Témesq)

OUPI

Akko ⊙

Jourdain

Lac de Tibériade

Mageddo ⊙

CANAAN GALILÉE

⊙ Yénoam
⊙ Beth Shan

Jaffa ⊙

⊙ Ourousalim — Hamath

▲ Mont Nêfo

Ascalon ⊙
Gaza ⊙

*Mer
Morte*

⊙ Dibon

Ras Kasroun ⊙

Raphia ⊙

⊙ Rabath Batona

Eaux de Râ   *Lac Sirbonis*   el-Arish ⊙   **NEGUEV**

Silé (Tjarou) ⊙

Pi-Ramsès ⊙   **Désert de Shour**

ÉDOM
(SEÎR)

« Route du Roi »

ÉGYPTE

⊙ Timma

SINAÏ   **MADIAN**

www.editionsarchipel.com

Si vous souhaitez recevoir notre catalogue
et être tenu au courant de nos publications,
envoyez vos nom et adresse, en citant
ce livre, aux Éditions de l'Archipel,
34, rue des Bourdonnais 75001 Paris.
Et, pour le Canada,
à Édipresse Inc., 945, avenue Beaumont,
Montréal, Québec, H3N 1W3.

ISBN 978-2-8098-0367-9

PREMIÈRE PARTIE

L'OMBRE DU RIVAL

1

Le vol du faucon

L e soleil lui-même était déjà cruel. Les faces et les corps des écuyers et lieutenants des Écuries royales, alignés dans la grande cour, à l'est du Palais royal de Ouaset[1], luisaient comme du bronze poli. Le bleu du ciel était aussi implacable que la justice divine.

Le spectacle n'était pas moins pénible.

Un homme agenouillé au milieu de la cour, les mains liées derrière le dos, venait d'entendre la sentence du maître des Écuries, le corégent Ramsès en personne : trente coups de fouet pour détournement des fonds alloués aux écuries.

Le premier coup de fouet claqua. La lanière en nerf de bœuf lacéra le dos du coupable. Le sang perla. La bouche du condamné s'ouvrit, mais aucun son n'en sortit. Il avait peut-être vingt-deux ans, mais il avait montré sa bravoure dans maintes opérations punitives contre les Shasous[2], en Amourrou. Il ne crierait pas.

Le deuxième coup de fouet traça une quasi-parallèle à la première lacération. La victime baissa la tête. Ni la douleur ni l'humiliation ne lui tirèrent plus qu'un râle rauque.

Les lieutenants frémirent. Ils connaissaient Horamès. Ils avaient partagé avec lui les rigueurs de la guerre et les plaisirs

---

1. Thèbes.
2. Les Bédouins de Palestine.

11

de la victoire, les danseuses et les bières des soirs de solde. La fraternité unit-elle donc les corps ? Ils ressentaient sur les leurs les coups cinglants de la lanière de cuir.

Au troisième coup de fouet, un filet de salive tomba de la bouche de Horamès, droit comme un fil à plomb, sans se décider à rejoindre le sol.

Plusieurs visages se crispèrent. Qu'avait-il volé ? Cent anneaux de cuivre ? Deux cents ? Mille ? Quel bien suprême ou quelle faute justifient jamais le supplice ?

Au cinquième coup de fouet, le torse du lieutenant déchu était tellement incliné que le fouet ne fit que l'effleurer. Plusieurs officiers se dirent que Horamès ne survivrait probablement pas à sa peine.

Les visages des spectateurs se levèrent : un faucon planait au-dessus de la cour. Il semblait presque immobile, symbole vivant du dieu Horus palpitant sur cette scène de justice.

Le justicier brandissait son fouet pour le sixième coup quand un messager accourut vers l'intendant adjoint des Écuries et, d'un ton fébrile, l'œil affolé, lui débita une information à l'évidence dramatique. L'intendant cria au justicier d'arrêter. Le bras armé du fouet se figea un instant, puis retomba. Le châtiment était suspendu. Les lieutenants s'étonnèrent, mais brièvement ; ils avaient deviné le motif de la grâce. Le pharaon Horemheb, alité depuis quelques jours, était donc parti pour le Grand Occident. C'était la seule explication à l'interruption du supplice. Le deuil royal l'interdisait.

Le faucon fila à tire-d'aile.

— J'ai l'immense chagrin de vous informer que notre maître, Amon incarné, le bien-aimé Horemheb, a quitté nos terres pour regagner son trône céleste, proclama l'intendant adjoint. Déliez le condamné.

Des lieutenants s'élancèrent pour relever et soutenir ce dernier, car il s'était écroulé au sol. Le médecin fut mandé et, en attendant qu'il vînt, les plaies furent lavées à la bière et l'on tendit à Horamès une gargoulette d'eau filtrée.

L'agitation régnait dans la caserne. La mort de Horemheb revêtait une tout autre dimension que l'état d'un lieutenant fouetté. Le pays changeait donc de maître. Et les Écuries royales aussi bien, car le successeur ne conserverait certainement pas cette charge.

Ce serait donc Ramsès. L'intendant adjoint s'était essuyé le visage et, ayant rajusté sa perruque, s'apprêta à gagner l'aile du palais où habitait le futur pharaon, afin de lui exprimer sa tristesse.

— Horamès est gracié ? demanda son second.

— Oui, répondit l'intendant adjoint avec humeur. Ce faucon… était un signe.

Les deux hommes échangèrent des regards sombres. Horamès avait été l'un des favoris du défunt monarque. Mais de là à conclure que l'âme du mort était venue suspendre le châtiment, il y avait un pas que même des hommes pieux hésitaient à franchir. Toutefois, vu le nom du lieutenant, qui signifiait « Horus l'a engendré », il était également difficile de passer outre à la coïncidence.

Personne n'avait prêté attention à une jeune femme qui, dissimulée derrière une porte entrouverte de l'intendance, avait assisté au supplice. Le visage de pierre sous les coups de fouet, tressaillant à chaque claquement de la lanière de cuir sur le dos du lieutenant, elle s'était brusquement dérobée après le sixième coup. Elle avait fondu en larmes et c'était courbée dans les sanglots qu'elle avait disparu.

Peu après, un messager du Palais vint emmener le lieutenant déchu on ne savait où.

Un messager à cheval !

Personne non plus n'avait prêté attention à un spectateur qui avait observé la scène du haut de la terrasse dominant la cour de la caserne. Un garçonnet de cinq ans.

À la nuit tombée, un petit groupe de clients dépités s'attardait devant la maison de danses proche de l'avenue du Grand-Fleuve. Situé au bord de l'eau, l'établissement portait un nom charmant, Le Palais d'Ihy. Il recevait d'habitude une jeunesse tapageuse et dorée, venue blanchir la nuit en buvant de la bière ou du vin tout en se rafraîchissant les yeux au spectacle de jeunes danseuses peu voilées. Mais ce soir-là, les portes étaient closes. Nulle musique de sistres ni de tambourins n'en franchissait les murs, nul lumignon n'y brillait. Mais que se passait-il donc ? Deux ou trois jouvenceaux s'impatientèrent et allèrent tambouriner sur la porte. À la fin, celle-ci s'entrouvrit et les clients reconnurent le visage de la tenancière, dame Ianoufar, « Lune de Nénuphar », sans perruque ni fard et l'expression mécontente.

— Préfères-tu la compagnie des chouettes à la nôtre, femme ? lança l'un des jeunes gens, d'un ton goguenard.

— Dans quel terrier vivez-vous donc, bande d'ichneumons, pour venir ainsi faire du fracas à ma porte ? Vous ne savez pas que le pharaon est mort ? Je n'ouvrirai pas de la semaine !

Ils se dévisagèrent, stupéfaits. Le pharaon était mort ? Isolés dans les bureaux et les études d'administration de la périphérie, ils n'en avaient rien entendu dire. Les hérauts n'annonceraient que le lendemain l'événement à son de trompettes.

— Sers-nous donc un pichet pour nous consoler, s'aventura à suggérer l'un d'eux.

— Vous voulez que la police vienne me mettre à l'amende ? rétorqua Ianoufar d'un ton furieux.

Et elle claqua la porte.

Point d'alcool, point de danseuses et un deuil national. Les aspirants fêtards regagnèrent leurs domiciles d'un pas morne.

2

L'incident d'une perruque tombée

L a perruque cérémonielle noire était tombée de la tête du garçon. Ou peut-être l'avait-il enlevée à cause de la chaleur régnant sur le bateau, lors du retour vers Ouaset, après les funérailles du pharaon Horemheb. À cet âge, le sens de l'étiquette était encore fragile chez les petits princes.

Et alors qu'il se penchait, le bras tendu vers l'eau, à la rambarde du premier navire du cortège fluvial, celui de l'héritier du trône, Ramsès Meryamon Menpehtyrê, dans l'espoir d'apercevoir des poissons, tous les dignitaires de la cour, embarqués sur les navires suivants, avaient découvert sa vraie chevelure. Ils n'avaient pu retenir leur stupéfaction.

Leurs regards ne s'étaient pas attachés au visage de l'enfant, exquise frimousse qui évoquait la fraîcheur d'une pomme, mais à ses cheveux – roux. D'un roux flamboyant, que la brise du Grand Fleuve faisait scintiller en les ébouriffant.

Quelques-uns l'avaient reconnu. Pa-Ramessou, le fils cadet de Séthi et petit-fils du prochain maître du pays de Horus, Ramsès Meryamon Menpehtyrê, était donc roux.

Roux ? Oui, la couleur dangereuse du dieu Seth. Le symbole de la violence, l'incarnation de la redoutable crinière solaire qui asséchait la terre. C'était extraordinaire, aux franges de l'impensable. Il n'y avait pas dans tout l'Empire dix personnes rousses. Des gens à cheveux jaunes, sans doute, oui, là-bas, à l'est, au

15

voisinage des épouvantables Hattous[1], mais roux, non. D'ailleurs, les ânes, les bœufs et les chiens roux étaient chassés des terres cultivées. Et les perruquiers avaient soigneusement dissimulé ce trait singulier : non seulement sa perruque était-elle de la couleur réglementaire, quasi noire, mais encore la mèche de l'enfance, qui dépassait tout aussi réglementairement du bandeau de tête, était-elle de la même couleur.

Et un jour, peut-être, ce garçon aux cheveux rouges régnerait sur l'Empire ?

Les marins aux voiles devinèrent bien qu'un incident agitait leurs sublimes passagers, car plusieurs d'entre ceux-ci avaient quitté l'ombre fraîche des cabines pour aller se poster à l'avant des navires et tenter d'apercevoir on ne savait quoi au juste. Mais entre-temps, l'une des dames de la cour s'était avisée de l'émoi déclenché par l'apparition du garçonnet sans perruque à la rambarde du navire de tête. Pa-Ramessou avait donc regagné la cabine et avait été dûment recoiffé de sa perruque noire, tout aussi dûment repeignée.

Les coiffeuses de la cour avaient d'ailleurs fort à faire depuis la mise au tombeau du sarcophage royal : dans la poussière du Haut Pays, les perruques devenaient grises au bout d'une heure. Et elles y perdaient également leur lustre. Mais on le savait bien dans leur profession : enterrement signifie triple charge de travail. Et tandis que les pleureuses s'échevelaient la crinière en s'égosillant, les perruquières passaient leur temps à peigner et lustrer ces coiffures confectionnées avec du crin de queue de cheval.

La surprise ne céda pas à la disparition du garçonnet.

À vrai dire, la rumeur d'un rouquin dans la famille princière courait depuis quelque temps, propagée par les domestiques, garçons de bains, maîtres des Garde-robes, esclaves du premier rang, allez savoir ! Mais personne n'avait pu le vérifier, perruque obligeant ; en effet, les membres de la famille régnante ne se montraient en public que coiffés.

— Ce garçon incarne donc parfaitement l'esprit du nom de son père Séthi, observa solennellement un dignitaire de la cour, le chef des scribes, passager du troisième des quatorze navires du cortège.

---

1. Les Hittites.

L'observation valait admonestation. Le dignitaire ne tolérerait pas d'allusions déplacées. Le nom de Pa-Ramessou à lui seul inspirait le respect : *râ*, c'était le globe solaire, *mes*, l'enfant royal, et *sou*, la plante de l'avenir. Le fils Pa-Ramessou était un gamin, mais un gamin royal.

— Seth est le dieu qui a sauvé le monde en transperçant de sa lance le serpent Apopis, ajouta le chef des scribes d'un ton encore plus sentencieux. Et c'est lui qui fait surgir les oasis dans le désert.

Il espérait prévenir de la sorte les commentaires graveleux sur le fait que le dieu Horus avait coupé les couilles de Seth pour se venger d'avoir été éborgné, au cours d'une bagarre céleste. Nul doute qu'après avoir daubé sur l'infortune de ce dieu à la tête bizarre, mi-renard mi-ichneumon, certains imprudents soulèveraient la question de la généalogie du rouquin et du reste de sa famille.

Les femmes ravalèrent donc les insinuations plus ou moins bienveillantes sur les origines brumeuses de la mère du phénomène, Thouy, Première Épouse de Séthi : n'était-elle pas originaire d'une province de l'Est ? Les personnes d'âge et d'expérience savaient bien, elles, que le *ka* des ancêtres pouvait se transmettre à leur descendance, au-delà de plusieurs générations. Le petit prince portait sans doute le *ka* d'un Hattou ou d'un Hyksôs, c'est-à-dire de barbares.

A-t-on aussi idée d'être roux !

Les bavardages feutrés dérivèrent ensuite sur le détail des funérailles, magistralement organisées par le grand-prêtre d'Amon et le prochain héritier de la double couronne du Haut et du Bas Pays. On évoqua évidemment le malaise du prêtre-lecteur, qui s'était interrompu un long moment dans la récitation des formules sacrées. Une défaillance du cœur, suggérèrent certains, car ce prêtre était bien âgé.

— L'émotion, rectifia le chef des scribes.

Dans la barque royale, assis à l'arrière de la cabine, entre sa sœur Thiyi et son frère aîné Pa-Semossou, le garçonnet prodigieux se tenait coi, impatient de rentrer à Ouaset. Son visage pâle, à l'ovale délicat, reflétait sa contrariété.

— Je voulais voir les poissons, dit-il.

— Des rebelles des profondeurs, bons à manger pour le peuple, laissa tomber Pa-Semossou.

À l'avant de la cabine, Ramsès et son fils Séthi échangeaient des propos inaudibles. À un certain moment, le grand-père tourna la tête et Pa-Ramessou lui trouva l'air fatigué. Ces funérailles avaient décidément été une épreuve physique autant que morale pour tout le monde. Pa-Ramessou s'y était ennuyé autant qu'il avait été suffoqué de poussière.

Personne à bord ne se doutait cependant que la chevelure du prince Pa-Ramessou serait l'un des détails les plus mémorables des cérémonies célébrant le départ du précédent pharaon, maître divin de To-Méry[1], pour la place de Maât, dans le Grand Occident.

Les rames des esclaves, sous les ponts, continuèrent de battre les flots bruns en cadence, avec la régularité du sang dans les vaisseaux du corps.

Personne n'a donc jamais prévenu les adultes que leur manière de parler aux enfants est ridicule ? Même un chat comprendrait qu'ils tentent de dissimuler la vérité.

Quand, au terme de leurs voyages d'aller et de retour qui avaient duré deux jours, les passagers du cortège eurent enfin remis pied sur les quais de Ouaset, Pa-Ramessou put juger aux mines de chacun, au Palais royal, que les lamentations des pleureuses et l'affliction qui durait depuis près de trois mois étaient pure hypocrisie.

— Ils ont l'air contents, souffla-t-il à son frère aîné, Pa-Semossou, en observant la foule des dignitaires, chambellans, scribes et autres qui, sourires melliflus et yeux énamourés, s'empressaient auprès de son grand-père, Ramsès.

Pa-Semossou mit l'index sur les lèvres, pour enjoindre le silence.

Mais les faits demeuraient. Jusqu'alors corégent et vizir du défunt Horemheb, Ramsès, prince héritier de Tout le Pays, serait bientôt le nouveau roi. Ainsi en avait-il été décidé par le monarque dont la dépouille gisait pour les siècles des siècles au fond d'une chambre décorée dans les profondeurs d'une syringe du Haut Pays. L'ancien général d'Akhenaton, le pharaon dont on ne parlait qu'à mots couverts, quand d'ailleurs on l'évoquait, était mort au bel âge de soixante et onze ans, après quelque trente

---

1. L'un des noms de l'Égypte à cette époque.

années de règne. N'ayant pas d'enfants, il avait désigné Ramsès pour sa succession.

Les familiers du prince régent se félicitaient donc de la proche accession au trône de leur protecteur, car elle présageait évidemment leur avancement.

— Horemheb n'était donc pas le descendant d'un pharaon? avait jadis demandé Pa-Ramessou à son précepteur, l'aimable Thïa, fils d'Amonouahsou, le scribe de la table royale, maître des Approvisionnements du Palais depuis Horemheb.

Âgé de douze ans de plus que son pupille, Thïa était spontanément aimé de tous en raison de son visage doux et de son esprit vif et sans malice.

— Non, mais c'était un homme de grand mérite, lui avait répondu ce dernier. Il a rétabli l'ordre dans le pays, il a exterminé les brigands et supprimé la corruption et les milices privées. Il a aussi restauré et consolidé le culte d'Amon et les autres cultes traditionnels.

Quelques explications habiles avaient résumé l'égarement d'Amenhotep le Quatrième, qui avait attribué une place excessive au dieu Aton, représenté par le disque solaire, ce qui avait contrarié les clergés du Haut et du Bas Pays. Peut-être Thïa répugnait-il à expliquer à son pupille que l'auguste incarnation d'Amon que représentait Horemheb était un plébéien originaire de Hout-Nesoût, dans le Moyen Pays, et qu'il avait été fidèle aux clergés traditionnels de la région. Pa-Ramessou savait qu'il ne fait pas bon poser trop de questions, mais il découlait donc de la réponse de Thïa qu'avant Horemheb le désordre régnait dans le pays. Il connaissait la liste des rois, enseignée par le précepteur : avant Horemheb avait régné Aÿ. Avant Aÿ, Toutankhamon. Avant Toutankhamon, Semenkherê. Avant Semenkherê, Amenhotep IV...

Lequel d'entre eux avait été responsable du désordre? Et pourquoi le culte d'Amon avait-il été affaibli? Pa-Ramessou avait décidé d'attendre une autre occasion pour élucider ces questions. Il s'en était autorisé une seule de plus, à son père cette fois :

— Horemheb est-il notre aïeul?

— Non. Il a désigné mon père comme successeur parce qu'il connaissait sa valeur.

Mais de qui donc Ramsès était-il alors le fils? Séthi avait considéré son fils d'un œil amusé et avait ajouté ces mots énigmatiques :

— La grâce d'Amon peut s'incarner dans l'être qu'il choisit indépendamment de ses ancêtres. Mon père est d'une famille de fonctionnaires du Moyen Pays. Son rang lui a été conféré par la grâce de Horemheb, inspiré par la sagesse d'Amon.

Ramsès n'était donc pas le fils de Pharaon. Il en découlait que lui, Pa-Ramessou, n'était pas de royale lignée.

Il en demeura pantois. Comment peut-on être prince et roturier à la fois ?

— Pourquoi Horemheb n'a-t-il pas eu d'enfants ?

Thouy lâcha une exclamation scandalisée et Thiyi se retint de rire. Pa-Semossou fit une grimace. Séthi, interdit, se résigna à avouer qu'il n'en savait rien.

Un cheval de bois monté sur des roulettes fixait le mur d'un air buté. Mais Pa-Ramessou n'était guère d'humeur à le promener dans les couloirs au bout d'une ficelle. D'ailleurs, ce n'était pas le moment.

L'ombre de l'aiguille de bronze sur le cadran solaire dépassait la troisième heure après midi. L'heure à laquelle le Palais, mouches comprises, faisait sa sieste. Pa-Ramessou connaissait son monde. Séthi, son père, et Thouy, sa mère, se retiraient chacun dans ses appartements, au premier étage, faisaient déposer sa perruque sur la catin au chevet de son lit et s'assoupissaient jusqu'à la quatrième heure. Thïa faisait de même. Après quoi, suivi de ses trois scribes, Séthi allait s'entretenir, dans les bureaux de l'aile est du Palais, avec les chefs de l'armée et des gouverneurs de province. Thouy et Thiyi recevaient les dames de la cour, mangeaient un fruit de saison, puis se rendaient aux bains avec ces dames. Pa-Semossou et Pa-Ramessou, eux, attendaient en compagnie de Thïa le retour de leur père, vers la sixième heure, pour gagner les bains à leur tour, se faire savonner, raser, masser et huiler le corps, poncer la plante des pieds et limer les ongles. Le souper était servi après cela. Certains soirs, Séthi allait seul chez Ramsès prendre le vespéral repas. Parfois Ramsès et sa première femme, la Grande Épouse princière Sâtrê, s'invitaient chez Séthi, et, dans ce cas, les mets étaient particulièrement raffinés, quartiers d'oryx grillés ou filets d'oie macérés dans la bière et cuits dans du vinaigre doux.

S'il ne faisait pas toujours la sieste, Pa-Semossou, lui, allait s'entraîner au tir à l'arc dans les jardins du Palais. Avec un arc taillé à sa mesure, évidemment, et de petites flèches, mais non moins redoutables pour autant : il avait un jour failli éborgner un jardinier. Pa-Ramessou était invité par son précepteur à faire aussi sa méridienne, mais il en éprouvait rarement le besoin. Sa grande distraction pendant que les aînés, c'est-à-dire la quasi-totalité des habitants du monde, dormaient pour digérer – car il l'avait déjà compris, on ne peut faire deux choses à la fois, digérer et penser –, était d'explorer le Palais subrepticement. Des caves, des cuisines et de la brasserie aux guérites des archers sur les toits, il avait tout visité et, plus d'une fois, s'étant égaré, il avait été ramené aux appartements royaux par un domestique. Peu de gens prêtaient attention à ce garçonnet fureteur et furtif comme un rat et, comme il gardait sa perruque en place, il ne risquait pas de retenir les regards : probablement un fils de fonctionnaire cherchant son chemin.

Ces territoires n'étaient pas des lieux de délices ; les sous-sols en particulier empestaient par endroits l'urine, d'humain ou de rat, sinon pire, le personnel n'ayant pas toujours le temps ou la discipline nécessaire pour courir à l'une des fosses d'aisance. Qu'importait, le plaisir du garçon était la découverte.

Il connaissait tout du Palais, les archives et les remises de pots et marmites, la fonderie de pointes de flèches et les écuries, les ateliers des scribes et la buanderie où l'on blanchissait le linge royal, et pas si royal, des quartiers des esclaves aux mystérieux sous-sols où fermentait une vie clandestine, principalement fornicatoire. Les premières fois qu'il avait surpris des gémissements de femme dans un entrepôt d'orge, il avait été bouleversé : devait-il courir au secours de la malheureuse ? Alerter des gardes ? Mais un regard coulé derrière la porte l'avait à la fois rassuré et décontenancé : couchée nue sur des sacs d'orge, la victime ne semblait pas trop mal en point ; elle tenait entre ses cuisses un homme qui la besognait en cadence, tout en lui pétrissant les seins, et sur les épaules duquel elle avait posé ses pieds. Une esclave et un quelconque contremaître. Pas de meurtre ni de quoi fouetter un âne. Le rugissement de l'homme l'avait toutefois laissé perplexe. L'acte inspirait-il tant de rage ? Le type du quidam aussi : sa couleur de peau était bien pâle pour un naturel du pays. Sans doute un prisonnier de guerre, un homme de l'Est, engagé au Palais pour ses compétences. Le personnel du Palais, Pa-Ramessou l'avait entendu dire par son père, comptait bien deux mille personnes, dont trois cents femmes. De temps en temps, leur sang chauffait, comme disait Pa-Semossou, à qui il avait confié son expérience et, comme ces gens n'étaient pas tous mariés, leurs humeurs chauffaient encore plus.

Depuis cette découverte, Pa-Ramessou passait indifféremment les chambres et recoins où des ahans caractéristiques le prévenaient d'activités sexuelles clandestines. Il n'était pas d'âge, il le savait, mais n'ignorait désormais plus grand-chose des anatomies respectives de la femme et de l'homme. N'ayant pas l'usage de ses instruments, il considérait ces affaires comme une faiblesse, sinon une affliction de l'âge adulte.

Il avait cependant fait, lui aussi, une bonne rencontre dans les sous-sols : un gros chat roux et vigoureux, qui longeait un jour un couloir en quête de rats ou de souris. À sa vue, l'animal s'était arrêté et l'avait dévisagé. Le garçonnet s'était accroupi pour lui parler. Le chat s'était approché à pas comptés et, de fil en aiguille, l'entretien avait fini dans des ronronnements et des caresses généreuses ; à la visite suivante, Pa-Ramessou s'était muni d'un quartier de canard dérobé dans le plat du déjeuner. Les rouquins s'entraidaient, c'était bien naturel.

Mais parmi les découvertes qui intéressaient le plus Pa-Ramessou, les bribes de conversations surprises au passage tenaient la première place. Certaines lui avaient ainsi appris que c'était pour d'obscures raisons sentimentales que vingt-cinq coups de fouet avaient été épargnés au troisième lieutenant des Écuries royales, Horamès, puni pour un détournement de fonds bien improbable. Pa-Ramessou n'avait rien compris d'autre aux chuchotements interceptés. Il fut d'autant plus intrigué qu'il avait bien perçu le nom de Horemheb. Auprès de qui pourrait-il démêler ces mystères ? Il remit la question à plus tard.

Deux ou trois jours après le retour des funérailles, il perçut la conversation suivante, dans le cellier :

— ... Maintenant, il faudra bien qu'ils prennent une décision en ce qui touche au petit prince.

— Mais où est-il, ce prince ?

— À Hetkaptah[1], à la garde des prêtres du temple de Ptah.

— Mais pourquoi?

— Je te l'ai dit, ses parents sont morts. C'est la nourrice qui a été le confier aux prêtres en présentant les sceaux en possession de la mère quand elle est morte.

— Et personne n'en a rien su jusqu'ici?

— Apparemment pas. J'ai entendu le directeur des Secrets des appartements du matin répondre au prêtre de Ouaset que le moment était mal choisi pour une pareille révélation et qu'il devrait attendre quelque temps avant de la communiquer au Premier chambellan de Sa Majesté.

— C'est une histoire incroyable! Et comment s'appelle ce prince?

— Ptahmose.

— Quel âge a-t-il?

— Six ans, ai-je entendu.

— Surtout ne te mêle pas de le répéter à qui que ce soit. On te ferait fouetter ou on t'enverrait dans une garnison d'Asie ou au pays de Koush[2]!

— Je ne suis pas fou. Et toi non plus, ne répète pas un mot de ce que je t'ai dit.

Des bruits de pas firent fuir Pa-Ramessou. Il était déjà à vingt coudées[3], caché dans une encoignure, quand la porte s'ouvrit. D'ailleurs, les deux hommes dont il avait saisi la conversation étaient partis dans l'autre sens. Il regagna le rez-de-chaussée en s'interrogeant sur cette étrange révélation: il y avait à Ouaset un petit prince du même âge que lui, qui s'appelait Ptahmose.

Un prince royal.

C'était bien plus intéressant que d'avoir vu fouetter un lieutenant des Écuries royales. Cependant l'information était contrariante: un prince royal serait un rival. Surtout s'il avait le même âge que lui.

---

1. Memphis.
2. Nom égyptien de la Nubie.
3. Une coudée thébaine valait 52 cm.

3

L'incarnation et le fantôme du rival

L e huitième jour après le retour de la cour à Hetkaptah, un génie turbulent s'empara du Palais. Dès l'aube, une fièvre inconnue de Pa-Ramessou fit vibrer l'air. Des essieux de chariots grincèrent alentour, bien plus nombreux que d'habitude, et les gonds des lourdes portes gémirent à leur tour, les murs de pierre s'emplirent des échos d'ordres lancés par les officiers chargés des divers services de l'administration royale, écuries, greniers et magasins, celliers, bureaux des scribes et des archives, garde-robes, buanderie... À la troisième heure après le lever du jour, les couloirs des appartements princiers résonnèrent du claquement des sandales de chambellans, secrétaires, scribes et domestiques. Les visiteurs de province affluaient dans la capitale, et ceux dont la faveur auprès de Ramsès n'était pas assurée tentaient d'en arracher une à Séthi, dans l'espoir d'un avancement, d'une prébende ou, faute de mieux, d'affermir leur position.

Même les mouches semblaient plus énervées qu'à l'accoutumée. Le couronnement approchait.

Pendant la semaine qui suivit, Séthi n'assista qu'à un ou deux soupers de famille, où il montra un visage exténué. Ce n'était certainement pas le moment de lui poser des questions sur un petit prince qui s'appelait Ptahmose.

Imbu de componction, l'instituteur qui dirigeait la classe d'âge de Pa-Ramessou, au collège royal ou *kep*, près du palais des

Femmes, consacra ses leçons à la signification du couronnement. Cela changeait des leçons d'arithmétique, de géométrie, de géographie et de religion. Il y avait là une vingtaine de fils de dignitaires de Ouaset, chambellans, premiers scribes, généraux et autres officiers de la Maison royale.

— Le pharaon Ramsès sera l'incarnation du dieu Amon sur la Terre. Il possédera l'éclat créateur de Rê, la force industrieuse de Ptah, la puissance protectrice de Horus et la vigilance combative de Seth. Comprenez-vous ?

Pa-Ramessou leva la main :

— Mais je croyais que Horus et Seth étaient ennemis ?

— Ils sont antagonistes, pas ennemis. Aucun des deux ne détruit l'autre. Leurs forces opposées s'équilibrent dans le ciel comme elles s'équilibreront dans la divinité du pharaon, sous l'égide du dieu Apep, Maître des Équilibres.

Pa-Ramessou songea alors que Horus avait sans doute vaincu Seth dans l'équilibre supposé de Horemheb, puisque celui-ci n'avait pas eu d'enfants. Une étincelle insolente alluma son regard. Le précepteur s'en avisa.

— As-tu une question à poser ?

— Oui. Si l'équilibre est rompu à l'avantage de Horus, la personne perd ses couilles[1] ?

L'instituteur fut pris de court par cette référence directe aux péripéties du panthéon. Dans la rumeur inquiète que le risque suscitait chez les gamins, assortie de suppositions goguenardes, il battit des paupières et chercha une explication convenable. Ce prince était décidément bien impertinent.

— L'équilibre ne peut pas être rompu. Apep y veille, répondit-il.

Mais son embarras n'était que trop visible. Et Pa-Ramessou n'en pensa pas moins.

Sur quoi, la perruque de l'élève princier glissa et, une fois de plus, l'instituteur vit les vrais cheveux de son pupille. Le souci assombrit son regard. Un garçon roux. Et prince. Nul doute, s'il parvenait jamais au trône, que son règne serait mémorable. Cependant, sur l'injonction de Thïa, qui assistait au

---

1. Allusion à un épisode de la mythologie égyptienne où, après avoir déjoué une tentative indécente de son oncle Seth, Horus, fils d'Osiris, lui coupa les testicules.

cours, comme d'habitude, Pa-Ramessou rajusta promptement sa coiffure.

À l'heure de la sieste, ce jour-là, Pa-Ramessou renonça à ses explorations des entrailles du Palais. On se bousculait dans les quartiers de l'intendance et les sous-sols et, la veille encore, il avait failli être écrasé par un sac de froment qu'un esclave avait maladroitement laissé tomber. Il limita donc ses incursions aux toits et terrasses du Palais et des bâtiments attenants, d'où il avait observé la flagellation du lieutenant Horamès. Vaste domaine. Le seul inconvénient était que les terrasses ne communiquaient pas entre elles, non seulement en raison de leurs différents niveaux, mais encore pour des raisons de sécurité. Il eût été ainsi impensable qu'on pût, des toits de l'une des ailes latérales, accéder à celui des appartements royaux et princiers et que les pieds d'un mortel se trouvassent de la sorte au-dessus du pharaon. Seuls les maîtres et fonctionnaires de la Garde-robe étaient ainsi autorisés à s'y rendre, eux seuls sachant à quel moment le monarque était absent de ses habitations.

Pa-Ramessou l'avait entendu dire une fois, mais il avait maintes fois mesuré l'écart entre ce que disaient les adultes et la réalité. Aussi gagna-t-il d'un pas décidé les anciens appartements royaux, au premier étage (en vérité, ils eussent dû se trouver au deuxième, mais le podagre Horemheb les avait fait déplacer au premier, trouvant les escaliers bien trop raides). Un formidable remue-ménage y régnait : après l'inventaire des biens du monarque disparu, dûment dressé par les scribes, on y préparait l'emménagement de son successeur. De nouveaux lits, bien sûr, de nouveaux sièges, d'autres coffres et d'autres luminaires. Des nuages de poussière ! Preste comme une souris, Pa-Ramessou se faufila jusqu'à l'escalier abrupt et gagna le toit. Il fut émerveillé : de sa vie, il n'avait jamais été aussi haut. Cinquante coudées ? Cent ? Il n'aurait su dire. Il découvrit le vaste paysage, au-delà des limites de la ville, jusqu'aux villages voisins, jusqu'aux temples de l'Ouest.

C'était donc sur ces étendues que régnait un pharaon. Et encore, il le savait, le pays était beaucoup plus grand, infiniment plus grand que ce qu'il embrassait du regard. De ces hauteurs, les humains sur l'esplanade paraissaient petits comme des mouches. Peut-être étaient-ils des mouches, en effet, et, lui, un rapace divin. Pa-Ramessou s'enivra d'espace. Une joie sans limites l'envahit, comme s'il était roi de ce Pays de Horus[1]. Il courut d'un bord à l'autre du toit, éperdu, s'arrêtant juste au bord, car aucune balustrade ne le protégeait du vide.

Soudain, il devint songeur. Il ne serait jamais roi de ce pays. Le prochain serait son grand-père, Ramsès. Et, après lui, son père, Séthi. Et, après celui-ci, son frère aîné, Pa-Semossou. Cela faisait beaucoup de temps. Il devint triste. Il quitta la Terrasse des Ivresses en esprit avant de reprendre l'escalier, contrarié et presque furieux.

Il erra dans le Palais comme un roi dépossédé. Il était retombé dans la réalité et c'était lui maintenant qui était petit. Dans le quartier des scribes, une terrasse s'ouvrait à son regard, entre deux colonnes. Il s'y aventura et découvrit l'esplanade devant la façade, et les soldats qui faisaient les cent pas le long des murailles. Nul enchantement n'en jaillit. Seules les hauteurs étaient enivrantes.

— Réjouis-toi dans ta céleste demeure, Amon, car voici que tu as enfanté un héritier terrestre pour ton royaume des Deux Terres.

La voix du grand-prêtre Pinedjem, debout devant son souverain, résonna entre les colonnes du temple d'Amon. Les sujets de la nouvelle Majesté, pressés en foule compacte devant les portes, entendirent l'invocation rituelle psalmodiée du maître suprême des dieux. Mais ils n'en virent rien : le sacre était une cérémonie secrète.

L'épaisse fumée d'encens montant des cassolettes bleuissait l'air.

Torse nu, le pagne blanc finement plissé ceignant ses reins jusqu'à mi-cuisse, la peau huilée lui prêtant les reflets du bronze, Ramsès semblait une statue. Son corps plébéien et charnu paraissait monumental, ses pieds massifs seraient désormais l'affirmation de la puissance royale, ancrée dans la terre des Deux Pays, et son masque large aux lèvres pulpeuses serait le visage de la divinité sur cette terre. À droite, à bonne distance du trône sur

---

1. L'un des noms de l'Égypte à cette époque.

lequel le souverain investi monterait bientôt, Sâtrê, l'épouse de Ramsès, son fils Séthi, Thouy, Thiyi, Pa-Semossou et Pa-Ramessou, les lointains parents de Horemheb et de Ramsès, observaient le cérémonial dans une immobilité si parfaite qu'on les eût crus déjà momifiés. À l'exception de Pa-Ramessou, les sens aux aguets et le visage comparable à la tête d'une souris qui guette un chat.

Flanqué de deux assesseurs, le grand-prêtre gravit les trois marches qui menaient au niveau d'une chapelle close, située exactement dans l'axe de la grand-salle, derrière Ramsès, qui s'était alors retourné : la chapelle était le *naos*, le saint des saints, le Centre de l'Univers. De part et d'autre de ses cloisons se dressaient des porteurs de torches. Les deux battants en étaient scellés. De sa canne cérémonielle, Pinedjem brisa le sceau. Deux verrous restaient à pousser.

Pa-Ramessou brûlait de curiosité. Quel trésor contenait la petite chapelle ?

— Le doigt de Sit glisse, clama le grand-prêtre en poussant le premier verrou. Le doigt de Sit glisse, répéta-t-il en poussant le second verrou. Le lien est rompu, le sceau est délié. Les deux portes du ciel s'ouvrent. Les deux portes de la terre sont décloses...

Plus vite ! songea Pa-Ramessou.

— ... Le cycle des dieux rayonne. Amon, le seigneur de Karnak, est élevé sur la grande place !

Les assesseurs ouvrirent chacun un battant. La statue en or du dieu suprême étincela dans sa chambre secrète, semblant frémir dans les palpitations des torches. Peut-être l'outrage de l'effraction déclencherait-il sa colère et le couronnement serait-il annulé, en dépit des discours conciliants du grand-prêtre. Le temple s'écroulerait, le monde serait annihilé...

Pa-Ramessou frémit aussi.

— Je suis celui qui monte vers les dieux, clama Pinedjem, presque pathétique. Je ne suis pas venu en ennemi du dieu. Je suis venu accomplir sa volonté.

Et il entra dans la chapelle. Nul ne perdait un seul de ses gestes. Il pérora, d'une voix qui monta vers l'aigu :

— La terre sigillaire est rompue, l'eau céleste est forcée, sois établi su. la grande place, Amon-Rê, seigneur de Karnak ! Ta couronne resplendit dans la gloire de ta puissance ! Tes beautés sont à toi, seigneur de Karnak et de l'univers !

Pinedjem se tourna vers l'assistance, saisie : il avait revêtu le masque d'Amon.

Chacun de ses deux assesseurs ajusta alors un masque différent : celui de droite, le masque de Horus, celui de gauche, le masque de Seth. Ils attachèrent au cou de Ramsès les insignes royaux du faucon et de l'abeille et lui remirent quatre sceaux, deux au nom de Geb, les autres au nom de Neith et de Maât.

Mais qu'était ce lit derrière la statue d'Amon ? se demanda Pa-Ramessou.

Les prêtres remirent à Ramsès une galette de terre et une hirondelle et lui reprirent les sceptres. Il se coucha sur le lit et les prêtres placèrent alors les sceptres sous sa tête, en chantant des formules que l'on percevait mal à l'extérieur de la chapelle.

Pa-Ramessou devina confusément que Ramsès mimait la mort. Celui qui avait été jusqu'alors le vizir et maître des Écuries royales n'existait plus. Le pharaon qui recevait l'esprit divin ne pouvait plus être un simple mortel. Mais la mort ne fut pas longue : Ramsès se releva et, au moment de franchir le seuil du saint des saints, un prêtre apporta des bols contenant deux fois sept plantes. Ramsès les huma l'une après l'autre et les décapita à l'aide de sa dague. Il accomplissait ainsi la destruction des forces ténébreuses.

Revenu dans la Maison de Vie, il fut alors entouré par douze prêtres, dont Pinedjem, portant toujours le masque d'Amon et tenant sur le bras une robe de lin rouge. Les célébrants aidèrent l'Élu à revêtir ce vêtement écarlate et se rangèrent auprès de lui. D'autres prêtres vinrent en procession lui offrir neuf oiseaux différents.

Les incarnations de Horus et de Seth retournèrent alors vers le *naos*. Deux couronnes étaient posées sur une table, au pied de la statue, une blanche et une rouge : Horus saisit la blanche, celle du Haut Pays, et Seth, la rouge, celle du Bas Pays. Les tenant à bras tendus, ils descendirent les trois marches et se dirigèrent vers Ramsès.

— Reçois la succession de ton père Osiris Ankh-Kheperou-Rê, aimé de Néfer-Kheperou-Rê, clama Horus.

— J'accueille l'âme de mon père Amon-Rê, répondit Ramsès. Je reçois la succession de mon père Osiris, fils d'Amon. L'aile de

Nekhbet me protège, les anneaux d'Ouadjyt me protègent, l'âme de mon père Amon-Rê descend en moi.

Pa-Ramessou était tellement pénétré par ces paroles qu'il sentit l'âme d'Amon-Rê s'infuser en lui. Son cœur se dilata. Il regarda, émerveillé, Horus poser la couronne du Haut Pays sur la tête de son grand-père, puis Seth y emboîter celle du Bas Pays. Horus tendit le sceptre à Ramsès et Seth lui remit le fléau. Deux insignes de la royauté, comme la double couronne.

Ramsès monta alors sur le trône.

Son petit-fils était en transe.

C'était lui qui avait été couronné. La puissance et la gloire l'emplissaient de félicité. Peu importait le moment où il serait investi, elles lui étaient promises. Il éprouva son initiation à la beauté éclatante du pouvoir. S'il l'avait voulu, il se serait envolé, comme le faucon Horus ou le vautour Nekhbet. Il en fut transfiguré.

Le pharaon Ramsès Ier descendit de son trône et se joignit au cortège que menait Pinedjem incarnant toujours Amon. La première image de lui que vit la foule amassée sur l'esplanade du temple fut celle d'un homme en robe rouge avançant d'un pas solennel entre les haies de soldats en armes. Suivaient son épouse et sa famille. L'on s'attendrit sur le petit garçon au visage grave encadré par les dames d'atour. Ensuite venaient les hauts fonctionnaires, le maître des Secrets des Deux Dames, les couronnes, le maître des Secrets du matin, le Premier scribe et ses adjoints, le maître de la Garde-robe, d'autres scribes, le général en chef des armées, des lieutenants... Le pharaon tout frais et son épouse montèrent sur un char doré, dont les chevaux allaient au pas. Plus d'une heure s'écoula avant que le défilé eût atteint les portes du Palais, pour participer au banquet quasi cosmique qui s'y tiendrait.

Il était alors deux heures après midi.

Recru d'émotions, ivre des parfums respirés pendant des heures, épuisé, Pa-Ramessou tombait visiblement de sommeil. Quelques échanges discrets entre sa mère et le maître adjoint de la Garde-robe permirent de négocier sa grâce et il monta discrètement à l'étage pour faire, de son plein gré cette fois, une sieste que n'interrompirent même pas les trompettes de la garde royale.

Quand il fut réveillé par l'un des scribes de la Garde-robe, afin de rejoindre son père et son frère aux bains, il eut l'impression d'être un autre.

Une détermination farouche, irrationnelle, envahit alors son esprit. Un jour, il le savait, il succéderait à Ramsès. Peu importait quand, il serait pharaon. Et il ne céderait jamais sa place à ce rival inconnu dont l'existence alimentait les conversations clandestines, ce prince qui avait le même âge que lui et qui s'appelait Ptahmose. À coup sûr un rejeton de l'ancienne dynastie.

Non, jamais!

Il serra les poings et les dents.

Aux bains, Pa-Semossou s'avisa de ses mauvaises dispositions. Et, tandis qu'il se faisait masser les jambes et le dos avec une huile camphrée, Séthi releva aussi la morosité butée de son fils cadet.

— Qu'est-ce que tu as?

— Je veux savoir qui est mon rival.

— Quel rival? Qu'est-ce que tu racontes?

Pa-Ramessou soutint le regard pourtant intimidant de son père.

— Ptahmose, répondit-il.

À l'expression contrariée de son père, Pa-Ramessou devina qu'il avait touché un point sensible. Pa-Semossou paraissait ahuri; à l'évidence, il ignorait tout du sujet. Séthi ne répondit pas. Les baigneurs achevèrent de le sécher, l'aidèrent à enfiler sa robe de lin et ses sandales, puis dispensèrent leurs soins à ses fils. Le maître de la Garde-robe surveilla le chef des perruques tandis qu'il recoiffait le futur vizir et ses fils, puis Séthi se dirigea vers la sortie et la salle des repas.

— Où as-tu entendu parler de Ptahmose? demanda-t-il en chemin.

— Je l'ai entendu, répondit Pa-Ramessou.

— Où?

— En allant chercher ma toupie, qui était tombée dans l'escalier.

Mensonge maladroit. Mais Séthi fut assez magnanime pour ne pas insister. Le fait était que Pa-Ramessou avait appris l'existence d'un rival et les circonstances importaient peu.

— Où est Ptahmose, père?

— Je l'ignore, fils. J'ignore même s'il existe vraiment.

— Il existe, père, répliqua le garçonnet d'un ton résolu, frisant l'impertinence. Il est à Hetkaptah, à la garde des prêtres du temple de Ptah.

— Mais que sais-tu d'autre, petit démon ? grommela Séthi d'un ton excédé, mais assez bas pour que personne de la suite princière ne pût l'entendre.

— Sa nourrice l'a confié aux prêtres et elle a présenté les sceaux en possession de la mère quand elle est morte.

Séthi s'arrêta pour fixer son fils de son regard le plus sévère.

— Mais qui le sait ?

— Père, le directeur des Secrets des appartements du matin a répondu à un prêtre de Ouaset que le moment était mal choisi pour une pareille révélation et qu'il devrait attendre quelque temps avant de la communiquer au Premier chambellan de Sa Majesté.

À ces précisions, Séthi sembla bouleversé. Mais il n'eut pas le temps d'approfondir les informations de son fils. Ils parvenaient, en effet, à la salle des repas et, ce soir-là, Sa Majesté et le grand-prêtre Pinedjem, ainsi qu'une vingtaine de prêtres du temple d'Amon, participeraient au repas, et il devait donc se composer une mine réjouie.

Il se joignit aux fonctionnaires qui attendaient l'arrivée de Sa Majesté. Dans de tels moments, Pa-Ramessou le savait, les enfants ne comptaient que par leur présence. Il ravala donc son humeur. Il sourit même avec une feinte candeur quand son grand-père vint lui caresser le menton avec la solennité qui sied à un dieu incarné.

Pareille distinction ne fut accordée ni à Pa-Semossou ni à Thiyi, leur sœur aînée. Un benjamin, Pa-Ramessou le savait, possédait le privilège de représenter la vigueur de la race ; il signifiait que la sève était toujours vigoureuse.

Dans une chapelle de la mémoire, comme il en existe tant au royaume de Ptah, enfouies sous les sables et vouées à l'oubli éternel, sinon à l'impiété des voleurs, les fresques sur les murs racontent une histoire ordinaire et pourtant touchante. Une jeune femme rencontra un jeune homme. Les fruits et la volaille sur les étals alentour indiquent que cela se passa dans un marché. L'artiste a représenté les dattes, les melons et le plumage des canards avec une fidélité minutieuse. La jeune femme est d'origine royale, comme en attestent son cartouche et la finesse extrême de ses attaches. Son buste est droit comme un jeune palmier et ses seins pareils aux melons, mais ô combien plus parfumés ! Elle est seule, son monde est tombé en poussière, à l'instar de sa dynastie, combattue par les prêtres, car son père voulut instaurer le disque solaire comme dieu unique. Impardonnable impiété, car dans son évidente unicité, la divinité est multiple. Toute créature qui prétendrait le nier se rabaisserait elle-même au rang excrémentiel de l'ignorance et à la condition criminelle d'une fiole de poison. Cette jeune femme, qui naquit dans le luxe le plus raffiné, vit désormais avec une dernière servante dans une maison de pauvre. Le jeune homme est un militaire, mais dans une formule subtile, son cartouche assure que, loin du champ de bataille, il est douceur et force, et son nom est « né de Horus », Horamès. L'artiste n'a pu représenter leurs échanges de regards, ni l'intimité nocturne, ni les caresses réciproques de leurs haleines ; il a simplement dépeint le geste qui les a rapprochés : le militaire a offert à l'inconnue une corbeille de pommes et c'est ainsi qu'elle a cessé d'être une inconnue. L'artiste n'a pas voulu imaginer les mots avec lesquels ils ont tissé et brodé le drap sur lequel ils se sont couchés. Il dit simplement que la jeune femme en a conçu un garçon et que son amant n'était pas au départ de la barque sur laquelle elle a prématurément gagné le Grand Occident.

4

Une conversation dans un souterrain

Le premier soin de Séthi, quand il eut accompli les servitudes physiques du lendemain matin, bu son bol de lait d'amandes et croqué sa galette au miel, fut d'informer le directeur des Secrets des appartements du matin du pharaon qu'il souhaitait s'entretenir avec lui. Il n'avait pas encore été intronisé vizir de son père ni reçu la bague et le collier au cours de la cérémonie qui se déroulerait plus tard dans la matinée. Mais son autorité virtuelle pesait déjà sur la cour, et le fonctionnaire Nahor ne pouvait se dérober au mandement.

De fait, il arriva promptement dans la salle des audiences du futur vizir.

— Mon maître exalté m'a convoqué, dit-il en s'inclinant.

— J'ai une question à te poser et elle est simple : es-tu au fait de l'existence d'un descendant de la famille régnante antérieure à notre vénéré Horemheb ?

Une lueur scintilla dans l'œil de Nahor.

— Je suis au fait, mon maître, de l'existence de quelqu'un dont on prétend qu'il descendrait de la famille d'Akhenaton.

— En as-tu parlé à mon père ?

— Je l'ai appris peu après le départ de notre vénéré Horemheb. À ce moment-là, le lumineux vizir, ton père, avait l'esprit occupé par la charge suprême qui l'attendait, et la mienne n'est pas d'encombrer les esprits célestes avec des ragots d'ichneumon comme il en court trop souvent dans les parages des demeures du ciel.

— Il serait soutenu par les prêtres de Hetkaptah, me dit-on.

Une autre lueur brilla dans l'œil de Nahor. À l'évidence, il était surpris que le futur vizir en sût autant, et Séthi, qui le comprit, s'amusa brièvement de ce qu'une rumeur dérobée par un gamin de cinq ans, Amon savait où, pût troubler un personnage aussi éminent. Il aurait été lui-même fort surpris s'il avait su qu'à cet instant Pa-Ramessou écoutait la conversation du fond du placard à rouleaux où il s'était caché. Une demi-heure plus tôt, en effet, il avait, de la terrasse des appartements princiers, entendu son père mander le directeur des Secrets ; devinant que Séthi essaierait de s'informer sur le mystérieux prince Ptahmose, il s'était dépêché de gagner cette cachette avant que la salle ne fût occupée.

— Je n'ai pu vérifier ce point, répondit Nahor, qui commençait à s'inquiéter. Mais je vais le faire avant d'évoquer cette rumeur devant mon céleste maître.

Façon de signifier qu'il en réfèrerait d'abord à son maître direct, Ramsès. Séthi ravala une impatience.

— Je vais requérir du céleste roi que je sois informé de tes recherches en même temps, rétorqua-t-il.

Réponse du berger à la bergère : si Nahor s'imaginait qu'il mènerait l'enquête à sa guise et à son rythme, il se fourrait le doigt dans l'œil. Il s'agissait d'une affaire dynastique et elle intéressait Séthi encore plus que son père Ramsès.

— Sait-on à la garde de qui est ce Ptahmose ? reprit Séthi.

Nouveau tressaillement de Nahor : Séthi était décidément bien informé ; il connaissait même le nom de ce prince. Mais qui donc lui avait fourni ces renseignements ? Il s'alarma.

— Je l'ignore, maître exalté.

— Je vais prier mon céleste père de hâter cette enquête, conclut Séthi sur un ton aussi raide que possible, mais sans offenser Nahor. Tu peux disposer.

Sur quoi un scribe de la Maison royale vint annoncer que le divin monarque souhaitait recevoir son fils. Séthi quitta incontinent la salle, suivi de son secrétaire et de ses scribes. Pa-Ramessou entrouvrit imperceptiblement la porte du placard et s'avisa qu'il ne restait plus qu'un seul scribe dans la pièce, un adolescent occupé à remplir les encriers. Peste du fâcheux ! Pa-Ramessou étouffait dans son réduit. Mais enfin, le jeune homme acheva sa tâche et sortit à son tour. Pa-Ramessou gagna prestement la terrasse, haletant, mais fort satisfait. Il avait deviné juste. Son père prenait l'affaire au sérieux.

꼭

La frustration est un fruit immangeable qui mûrit dans des cavernes souterraines et donc infernales, sur des arbres crochus. Dédaigné des hyènes elles-mêmes, il finit par choir, toujours hors de saison, quand il est trop mûr. Il éclabousse alors les gens alentour de ses glaires fétides et les rend mystérieusement malgracieux. Pa-Ramessou en tâta.

La vie suivit le cours que les saisons et les cérémonials prescrits par les humains, toujours les mâles, avaient imposé. Une semaine après le couronnement de Ramsès, son fils avait été nommé vizir et corégent et avait reçu le collier d'investiture.

Séthi avait alors été absorbé par les innombrables cérémonies et banquets. Tous les gouverneurs et les grands-prêtres de province, du nome[1] de Khnoum[2] et des frontières de Koush aux nomes du Bas Pays et aux rivages de la Grande Verte, affluaient à Hetkaptah. Leur absence eût signifié qu'ils n'existaient pas. Mais leur présence offrait des chances d'avancement. Aussi n'y avait-il plus un lit de libre à Ouaset et, quand l'aube se levait, les temples et les quartiers des scribes semblaient changés en dortoirs.

Thouy et Thiyi passaient le plus clair de leur temps à s'occuper de leurs atours et en compagnie des épouses des visiteurs.

Pa-Semossou, enfin, était devenu invisible : dès que ses cours avec le précepteur étaient achevés, il courait rejoindre les fils des mêmes visiteurs pour se livrer à des compétitions de tir à l'arc et, comme l'un des jouvenceaux avait failli éborgner un garde, Séthi avait donné l'ordre que ces joutes se fissent à bonne distance des habitations.

Pa-Ramessou déjeunait seul la plupart du temps. Il n'avait personne d'autre à qui parler que son précepteur Thïa et s'ennuyait ferme. Doté d'une nature prévenante, Thïa s'évertuait à arrondir les angles de la vie ordinaire, de crainte qu'ils ne blessent les gens

---

1. District.
2. Nom égyptien de l'île d'Éléphantine.

et notamment son pupille. Autant dire qu'il était porté à mentir par devoir autant que par sollicitude. Chaque fois que Pa-Ramessou effleurait le sujet de Ptahmose, le précepteur trouvait un faux-fuyant pour éluder le sujet.

Sur quoi survint la fête d'Opet[1], célébrant la visite du dieu Amon à son Harem du Sud, et Séthi disparut de nouveau pendant plusieurs jours.

Tout cela était bel et bon, mais rien n'avait été fait pour tirer au clair le mystère du prince Ptahmose.

Et Pa-Ramessou replongea dans les mystères du Palais.

Nul autre ne lui était offert. Le Palais était son domaine, mais aussi sa prison. Il ne pouvait en sortir pour aller explorer la ville voisine. Une aussi longue absence déclencherait la plus folle inquiétude et le soumettrait à la surveillance ininterrompue d'une horde de scribes, sans un moment de répit.

Le premier jour, les ragots ne lui apprirent rien qui méritât d'être inscrit sur les rouleaux des scribes. La fille aînée du second prêtre du temple de Khnoum s'était éprise du premier lieutenant des archers et forniquait avec lui dans les jardins du Palais, le gouverneur du nome de Ouaouât passait le plus clair de ses nuits dans les maisons de danses de la ville en compagnie de filles à peine nubiles et y dépensait des fortunes, le Premier scribe du gouverneur du nome d'Ipet-Sout vivait en ménage avec le deuxième scribe...

Les adultes se doutent peu du caractère dérisoire, pour un enfant, des racontars dont ils font leurs délices, surtout quand ils ont trait à des incartades sexuelles. Un enfant sait mieux que ne le soupçonnent ses aînés, ou que lui-même ne s'en souviendra plus tard, ce qu'il en est des choses du sexe, même s'il n'en a pas l'emploi : ce sont pour lui des attifets de l'âge, et il en mesure les débordements d'un œil cruel et clair. S'ils y éprouvent des émois, grand bien leur fasse. Les minauderies de la donzelle et les airs farauds de l'énamouré lui paraissent aussi drôles que les poursuites frénétiques d'un chat après une souris, à cette différence

---

1. Fête qui célébrait la crue du Nil, en septembre, et durait vingt-trois jours.

près que les rôles y sont plus ambigus. Il avait assez observé, par exemple, les momeries d'une certaine servante du service des Perruques des princesses, sa mère et sa sœur, à l'égard d'un robuste commis de la Garde-robe paternelle, pour n'en rien ignorer. Donc les infractions à un code qu'on ne lui avait pas encore enseigné, mais dont il devinait instinctivement les injonctions, lui paraissaient ridicules. Ce qu'il voulait, lui, c'était savoir qui était vraiment Ptahmose et où il se trouvait.

Cette idée fixe lui avait aiguisé les sens. Mais il ne décelait pas la moindre mention du rival, réel ou imaginaire, dans les bribes de conversations qu'il piquait au hasard de ses pérégrinations dans les couloirs et de ses indiscrétions.

Le troisième jour, une découverte lui fit momentanément perdre le fil de ses recherches. S'étant aventuré dans les sous-sols de la caserne, qui communiquaient avec le Palais par un couloir unique, il tomba sur des bruits de conversation qui annonçaient une réunion de plusieurs hommes. Le rythme des échanges, un fumet de ragoût de viande à l'oignon et des glouglous indiquaient que la rencontre se faisait autour d'un repas. La porte de la salle où se tenaient ces agapes était entrouverte. Prudemment, Pa-Ramessou glissa un œil entre les gonds : six hommes assis par terre, en tailleur et torse nu, autour d'un plateau.

— Encore un peu de bière ?

— Je veux bien.

— Il faudra faire un sacrifice à Horus. Le vol du faucon a fichu une fameuse trouille au général.

— Oui, tu m'as dit.

— Il est ravi de te réintégrer.

— J'ai été innocenté.

— Innocenté ou pas, tu n'aurais pas été réintégré sans l'ordre du nouveau vizir, Séthi.

L'ouïe de Pa-Ramessou se fit plus fine que celle d'une souris dans son trou.

— Tu ne veux pas nous dire le secret de ta disgrâce ?

— Je vous le dirais bien, mais il n'y en a pas d'autre qu'une infâme délation.

Un silence.

Pa-Ramessou scruta les convives et l'évidence lui sauta aux yeux : le dos qu'il apercevait portait plusieurs balafres. Des cicatrices encore fraîches, qui s'atténueraient sans doute avec le temps, mais qui étaient pour le moment bien visibles. Cet homme était donc le lieutenant des Écuries qu'il avait vu fouetter plusieurs semaines auparavant.

— Horamès, il n'y a peut-être pas de secret, mais comme tu es notre collègue et que nous t'aimons, nous devons te dire qu'il y a des rumeurs.

— Au nom de notre amitié, je vous prie de les garder pour vous. Je ne veux pas les entendre, répliqua l'autre avec détermination. Si je les écoutais, Herou, ce serait comme si je les approuvais.

Un long silence suivit.

— Je vous remercie de ce repas et de votre accueil, reprit Horamès en se levant. Maintenant, j'ai à faire avec le dressage des poulains.

Il saisit son baudrier, se leva, gagna la porte et sortit sans voir le gamin qui l'avait épié ; en effet, un groupe de servantes venait en sens inverse, portant des paniers de linge à blanchir, et le lui déroba à la vue. Le couloir redevint désert et Pa-Ramessou se retrouva seul. Il coula un regard entre les gonds. Les cinq autres lieutenants des Écuries restaient assis, sirotant des fonds de bière d'un air morose.

— Il ne pourra pas nier éternellement ces rumeurs, dit l'un d'eux.

— Si, pourtant. On finira par les oublier avec le temps. Son attitude est sage.

— Crois-tu que le pharaon les connaisse ?

— C'est lui qui a décrété le pardon.

— Ça ne veut pas dire qu'il connaisse les rumeurs. Il a décrété le pardon parce qu'il a compris que Horamès avait été victime d'une délation calomnieuse. Mais il ne connaît peut-être pas la véritable raison de la délation.

— C'était la vindicte du général Péhor. Il était le confident de Horemheb et ne s'est jamais consolé que ce pharaon n'ait pas eu d'enfants.

— Tais-toi, Noussès, les murs ont des oreilles.

— Je peux me taire, moi, mais on ne peut pas faire taire la vérité. Horamès avait été chargé de donner des enfants à l'Épouse royale, Moûtnedjmet, la fille du pharaon Aÿ. Il ne l'a pas fait. La dynastie de Horemheb aurait conservé le trône. Péhor aurait été vizir. Il a perdu toutes ses chances. Et tout ça, parce que la semence de Horamès n'a pas fécondé l'épouse de Horemheb.

— Tais-toi, te dis-je !

— Serais-tu le serviteur du mensonge ? Ou bien la vérité serait-elle un crime ? Nous savons, nous, que pendant son séjour à Het-kaptah, Horamès s'est épris d'une petite-fille d'Akhenaton, Néferneferourê, et qu'il l'a fécondée…

— Par le dieu Thot, ferme ta bouche !

— … et qu'un garçon est né de leur union. Vous connaissez même le nom de ce garçon : Ptahmose.

— Si quelqu'un entendait jamais cette conversation, nous finirions en pâture d'Apopis !

Le cœur de Pa-Ramessou battit à se rompre dans sa poitrine. Horamès était donc le père de Ptahmose.

— Tout ça, reprit le lieutenant bavard, celui qui s'appelait Noussès, n'aurait pas grande importance si les prêtres du haut en bas de ce pays n'étaient mécontents de voir sur le trône un homme qui ne possède pas une goutte de sang royal et qui ne peut donc pas être divin. Ils s'intéressent donc à ce prince de sang qui s'appelle Ptahmose et rêvent peut-être de l'élever au trône. Si vous croyez que ces rumeurs vont s'éteindre d'elles-mêmes, vous vous trompez.

— Sans doute, sans doute, mon bon ami ! coupa un autre militaire. Tu oublies cependant que le pouvoir de Horemheb était basé sur notre soutien, comme l'est celui de Ramsès. Nous avons partie liée avec le présent pharaon et nous n'avons aucun intérêt à divulguer des histoires sur l'existence d'un prince de la précédente dynastie. C'est sous les règnes d'Akhenaton et du petit Toutankhamon que ce pays a failli se disloquer comme une vieille charrette. Voilà pourquoi nous te demandons de fermer ton clapet.

— De plus, observa le lieutenant qui s'appelait Herou, nous ne voudrions pas assister à ta flagellation dans la cour de la caserne des écuries.

— Voulez-vous que je vous dise quelque chose ? rétorqua l'indiscret Noussès. Si j'étais à votre place, je me demanderais si je ne cours pas le risque d'être puni parce que j'aurais manqué de révéler au vizir l'existence d'un prince de l'ancienne dynastie.

L'argument leur cloua le bec un moment.

— Mais que proposes-tu de faire ? demanda l'un des contra-dicteurs.

— Je ne propose rien pour le moment, je réfléchis. Et je ne me comporte pas comme une femme qui craint le bâton de son mari.

Il se versa un plein gobelet de bière.

— Moi, dit un autre militaire, je proposerais de garder la tête froide. Tu l'as toi-même reconnu, Herou, ce ne sont que des rumeurs. Les rumeurs sont dangereuses. Nous sommes comme des enfants qui jouent avec des scorpions.

Pa-Ramessou regarda instinctivement ses pieds.

— Ah ! Ah ! écoutez la sagesse incarnée ! ricana Noussès. N'est-ce pas le grand-prêtre du temple de Ptah qui a révélé lui-même à notre ami Herou l'existence du prince Ptahmose et qui a précisé sa paternité et l'identité de la mère ? Allons, mes amis, assez tourné au tour du pot, dit-il en se levant.

Il était déjà à la porte quand il s'arrêta pour lancer à ses camarades :

— À la place de Horamès, je m'inquiéterais d'une chose.

— Laquelle ? demanda un militaire.

— Que ces prétendues rumeurs ne se répandent en si haut lieu que l'existence même du prince Ptahmose soit menacée. Ne l'oubliez pas, il peut quand même devenir un prétendant au trône.

Pa-Ramessou n'en entendit pas davantage. Il décampa, fou de terreur. Sa course ne s'arrêta que dans un escalier qui le ramenait à la lumière, quand il fut à bout de souffle, les jambes flageolantes.

5

La visite de la dernière servante

L e royaume s'organisait enfin dans la lumière neuve du pharaon. Les potentats de province étaient retournés chez eux,
après s'être gobergés et assurés de conserver leurs privilèges ou
d'en avoir acquis de nouveaux ; les prêtres avaient consolidé leurs
pouvoirs et obtenu de nouvelles terres ; les commandants des
places fortes du Haut et du Bas Pays pouvaient regagner leurs
casernes de Knoumsekhem ou de Ta Sny et dire qu'ils avaient vu
le pharaon et baisé sa sandale, et qu'il avait, dans sa suprême
sagesse, confirmé leur autorité.

La vie reprenait son rythme et Séthi, son rôle de père de
famille.

Le premier soir qu'il dîna à la maison après son entrée en fonc-
tions fut le surlendemain du jour où Pa-Ramessou avait surpris la
conversation entre les lieutenants des Écuries. Il en était encore
bouleversé. Lèvres scellées, mais regard de feu, il ne détachait
pas ses yeux de son père. À la fin, celui-ci s'en avisa.

— Que me dit donc mon cadet ? demanda-t-il, paterne et
souriant.

— Les semaines ont passé, père chéri.

— Ta sagesse a donc crû.

— C'est à toi d'en juger, père chéri.

Formules convenues, dûment enseignées par le précepteur.
Séthi hocha la tête, satisfait. Mais il était trop fin pour ne pas
comprendre que le regard de son cadet recelait une demande. Il

l'interrogea du sien : pas de doute, Pa-Ramessou avait quelque chose à dire.

— As-tu un souci ?

— Je voudrais toujours savoir ce qu'il en est du prince Ptah-mose.

Séthi perdit son expression bonhomme.

— Ah, mais oui. J'avais chargé le directeur des Secrets de s'en enquérir... Puis il y a eu tous ces événements. Je vais le relancer.

— Ptahmose pourrait être un prétendant au trône, père chéri.

Séthi ouvrit de grands yeux.

— Écoute, on n'est même pas sûr de son existence, on ne connaît ni son père ni sa mère...

— Le père est le lieutenant des Écuries Horamès, père, et la mère était la princesse Néferneferourê.

Une guêpe aurait piqué le vizir Séthi que son sursaut n'aurait pas été plus soudain.

— Horamès ? répéta-t-il. Horamès ? Lui ? Mais comment sais-tu tout cela, petit diable ?

— J'écoute, père chéri. Les gens parlent quand ils se croient seuls et je suis l'oreille des murs.

— Mais où écoutes-tu ?

— Partout.

Il leva un regard effronté vers son père :

— Et pourquoi l'épouse de Horemheb était-elle stérile ?

— Mais tu en sais plus que le chef de la police lui-même ! s'écria Séthi.

Les éclats de voix avaient attiré l'attention de Pa-Semossou et du Premier scribe, qui se tenaient à distance respectueuse. Ils observèrent le père et le fils, engagés dans une conversation apparemment importante. Mais sur quoi ?

— De même qu'il y a des yeux qui ne voient pas, dit Séthi, il y a des ventres qui ne conçoivent pas.

Séthi semblait pensif.

— Si ce que tu dis est vrai, fils, reprit-il, il faut le vérifier. Demain, nous irons à Hetkaptah.

Soudain content, Pa-Ramessou enleva sa perruque et se gratta le crâne. Admiratif et stupéfait, Séthi considéra ce brin d'homme aux cheveux flamboyants. Peut-être le dieu Seth avait-il été pareil, quand il avait eu son âge... Mais que sait-on de l'enfance des dieux ?

Excepté le voyage en bateau pour les funérailles de Horemheb, c'était la première fois que Pa-Ramessou sortait de Ouaset. S'efforçant de garder l'équilibre sur un cheval bai, suivant son père, encadrés par deux officiers des Écuries et escortés par le Premier scribe, deux assesseurs et un détachement de fantassins, ils venaient, Séthi et lui, de débarquer à Hetkaptah au terme d'une longue journée de voyage. Le directeur des Secrets du matin ne faisait pas partie de l'expédition, ce qui constituait un désaveu tacite : il avait trop traîné à élucider l'affaire dont il était chargé. Accueillis au son des trompettes par le gouverneur et le général de la garde royale de la ville et quatre officiers, père et fils prirent la direction de l'un des palais, qui avait été préparé pour la circonstance. Quand il en avait entendu parler à l'occasion, Pa-Ramessou avait appris que la ville était considérée comme la charnière des Deux Pays : celui qui la tenait commandait la vallée. Son père le lui confirma :

— C'est ici, mon fils, que l'on forge les armes de nos soldats, les sabres, les lances, les boucliers, c'est ici que l'on construit les chars.

Au loin, Pa-Ramessou distingua la pyramide de l'antique pharaon Pépi Ier, puis le cortège parvint au Palais. Un soldat joignit les deux mains pour inviter le petit prince à y poser le pied, cependant qu'un autre soutint le cavalier pour l'aider à poser pied sur un escabeau.

Une foule se forma pour assister à l'arrivée des visiteurs et capter une image de leur apparence. Elle en eut à peine le temps : ils disparurent prestement derrière une haie de fantassins, puis dans les bâtiments royaux. Le ciel d'Occident se teintait de rouge éclatant, où, telles des paillettes d'or, scintillaient les poussières venues du désert, et celui d'Orient s'était tendu d'indigo. Le père et le fils prirent leurs quartiers, les baigneurs avaient fait chauffer de l'eau dans la piscine des bains et, quand les voyageurs eurent été rafraîchis, le chambellan vint demander au vizir s'il souhaitait des danseuses et des chanteuses pour agrémenter son dîner.

— Non, répondit Séthi, nous nous lèverons tôt, ces artistes incitent à veiller. Fais prier le gouverneur de s'asseoir à ma table. Il sera mon seul invité. Et seul mon Premier scribe sera présent.

Le chambellan hocha la tête et se confondit en formules de révérence.

Une demi-heure plus tard, les quatre convives étaient assis. Pa-Ramessou ouvrit grand ses oreilles. Les domestiques vinrent présenter les bols, les aiguières d'eau parfumée et les serviettes de lin, et les dîneurs se lavèrent donc les mains.

Séthi avait choisi le menu : une salade de poireaux à l'huile, des filets de poisson de la Grande Verte, puisqu'on était à proximité, frits dans l'huile ; seuls les prêtres s'étant interdit le poisson, animal inférieur, il n'y avait pas lieu de s'en priver. Suivraient des quartiers de canard grillés, du blé cuit et des dattes fraîches. Comme boissons, du vin et de l'eau de puits filtrée au sable.

— Excellence, déclara Séthi quand le gouverneur se fut assis devant lui, ceci est une visite officieuse, et je ne souhaite pas qu'elle soit inscrite dans vos registres sous un autre motif qu'une visite à la forteresse du Mur blanc.

— Ainsi en sera-t-il, maître vénéré, répondit le gouverneur.

— Maintenant, dis-moi : es-tu au fait de l'existence d'un descendant de la dynastie des révérés Amenhotep qui serait à la garde des prêtres de Ptah ?

Le regard de Pa-Ramessou se plaqua sur le visage du gouverneur comme une sangsue sur le pied d'un homme.

— Bien sûr, mon maître. C'est un garçon de six ans qui se nomme Ptahmose. Il est le fils de Néferneferourê, la cinquième des filles du dernier des Amenhotep, celui qui se faisait nommer Akhenaton, et d'un lieutenant des Écuries à Ouaset, Horamès.

Séthi en fut abasourdi : le gouverneur avait répondu d'emblée, comme si c'était la chose la plus connue du monde.

— Et tout le monde le sait ? reprit Séthi.

— Le garçon intéresse peu de monde, mon maître. N'avons-nous pas eu le glorieux Horemheb ? Et son choix inspiré de son successeur ne s'est-il pas porté sur ton divin père ? Qu'importe l'existence du rejeton d'une lignée dont le dernier représentant laissa le noble Pays de Horus en proie à la rapine et à la dissension ?

Le gouverneur essuya avec un linge ses lèvres, brillantes de l'huile des poireaux, et vida son gobelet de vin. Pa-Ramessou, lui, attendait la suite de la conversation : son père tolérerait-il un rival de son fils ?

Les serviteurs déposèrent sur la table un grand plat de filets de poisson et regarnirent les verres des adultes ; Pa-Ramessou n'avait que tâté du vin.

— Et pourquoi les prêtres de Ptah lui ont-ils accordé leur protection ? demanda Séthi.

— J'ignore leurs motifs exacts, mon maître. Je n'ai que des hypothèses. Ils ont recueilli l'enfant à sa naissance, il y a six ans. Le divin roi Aÿ était mort sans descendant mâle. Horemheb était également mort sans progéniture. Ils se sont peut-être dit que, dans le cas où le trône céleste resterait sans prétendant, il ne serait pas malvenu de proposer un héritier qu'ils auraient formé et qui régnerait un temps sous la tutelle de leur choix.

Un léger sourire accompagna ces propos. Pa-Ramessou frémit : il avait deviné juste : Ptahmose serait un rival. Les prêtres voulaient que le trône fût occupé par le membre d'une lignée royale.

Séthi semblait ruminer ces informations.

— Le divin Horemheb connaissait-il l'existence de ce garçon ?

Le gouverneur chercha ses mots.

— Puis-je me permettre de demander si mon maître connaît les faits ? demanda-t-il d'un ton confidentiel.

— Peut-être pas tous, répondit Séthi.

— Horamès fut le rival de ton divin père au commandement des Écuries. Horemheb y avait mis une condition : qu'il fécondât son épouse.

Exactement ce que Pa-Ramessou avait entendu dans les sous-sols du Palais de Ouaset. Il ne put retenir un geste d'impatience, qui n'échappa pas à son père.

Séthi sirota son vin d'un air méditatif.

— Le plus sage, me semble-t-il, est d'aller voir ce garçon demain.

— Sans prévenir les prêtres, j'imagine ? suggéra le gouverneur d'un air entendu.

— En effet, admit Séthi avec un rire bref.

Le dîner s'achevait. Séthi donna congé au gouverneur et rendez-vous pour le lendemain matin aux premières heures.

Pa-Ramessou eut les plus grandes peines à s'endormir.

La statue qui dominait le parvis, devant la colonnade du temple, mesurait bien trente coudées. Mais en réalité, elle n'avait pas de dimensions. Elle était aussi grande que l'humain peut s'imaginer le surhumain. Elle représentait le dieu Ptah, créateur du monde par la pensée et par le verbe, gardien tutélaire de Het-kaptah et inventeur des techniques. Pa-Ramessou fut saisi, effrayé et séduit. Ptah était beau, il était la plénitude et la force. Les dieux représentaient le pinacle de la beauté.

Il ne put s'attarder dans sa contemplation : ayant contourné le temple, le cortège du vizir parvenait aux habitations du grand-prêtre qui, à Hetkaptah, s'appelait Doyen des maîtres artisans. Les fantassins aidèrent Séthi et les autres cavaliers à mettre pied à terre. Séthi avança le premier, tenant son fils par la main et flan-qué du gouverneur. Sous les frondaisons du jardin, les scribes penchés sur leurs tablettes levèrent la tête et, devinant quelque événement important, glissèrent leurs calames derrière l'oreille. Le Premier scribe de l'équipage de Séthi alla prévenir la maison du grand-prêtre que le vizir, de passage à Hetkaptah, désirait s'en-tretenir avec le maître des lieux.

Celui-ci s'empressa à la rencontre de ses visiteurs, les bras levés au ciel ; il s'appelait Khouper Ptah et, s'il n'en avait été une vieille connaissance, il avait été néanmoins l'un des courtisans les plus assidus auprès de Ramsès et de Séthi lors de son passage à Ouaset, pour les fêtes du couronnement. Séthi lui donna l'acco-lade et lui présenta son fils.

Pa-Ramessou parcourait les parages de son œil inquisiteur, à la recherche de n'importe quel garçon d'à peu près son âge. En vain.

Séthi donna l'ordre d'offrir à Khouper Ptah les présents qu'il lui apportait : des sacs de froment, deux jarres de vin, un coffret d'encens… Le grand-prêtre se confondit en remerciements, pour la plupart adressés au dieu qui lui avait ménagé une aussi pro-pice journée, puis à la munificence du vizir, qui reflétait l'infinie générosité du pharaon, son père. Il invita ses visiteurs à entrer dans sa maison. Des serviteurs apportèrent du vin et le versèrent dans les gobelets.

Pa-Ramessou s'impatientait.

Un silence annonça que le sujet de la visite ne tarderait pas à être abordé.

— Dans ta compassion, déclara Séthi, tu as accueilli le rejeton d'une dynastie disparue.

Khouper Ptah avait-il été prévenu de l'objet de la visite?

— Il est exact, exalté vizir. Il y a un peu plus de cinq ans, une servante éplorée est venue nous supplier de prendre en charge le petit enfant qu'elle tenait dans les bras, dont la mère venait de mourir et qui n'avait plus de famille au monde. Sa détresse était évidente. Elle ne pouvait prononcer un mot qui ne fût baigné de larmes. Ma femme a spontanément déféré à ses vœux et confié l'orphelin à la nourrice de mes enfants. J'ai demandé à cette femme qui étaient les parents de l'orphelin. Elle m'a répondu à contrecœur: « J'étais la dernière servante de la princesse Néferneferourê. » Le nom m'a évidemment intrigué. Ç'avait été celui de la cinquième fille du pharaon Amenhotep le Quatrième, celui qui avait bouleversé notre céleste famille pendant tant d'années. J'ai alors demandé à cette femme si elle avait des preuves de ses dires. Elle a tiré d'une sacoche des sceaux royaux, un bracelet, une bague, un peigne et divers objets qui semblaient le prouver, car ils étaient inscrits du nom de cette princesse. « Je ne vous les confie pas, a-t-elle dit, c'est mon seul héritage et tout ce qui me reste comme bien. Ma maîtresse me les a donnés. J'en ai déjà vendu pour payer les embaumeurs. »

Khouper Ptah observa une pause. Pa-Ramessou ravala sa salive. Séthi, le gouverneur et le Premier scribe semblaient saisis par la révélation.

— Je me suis demandé si ces objets ne provenaient pas d'un vol. Les pilleurs de tombes, hélas, ne cessent jamais leurs maudites déprédations. Mais à quoi eût servi de revendiquer une origine royale pour cet enfant? Cette servante avait parlé d'embaumeurs. Leur tâche n'était certes pas achevée et je leur ai rendu visite en compagnie de la servante. « Que vous a-t-elle donné en paiement? », leur ai-je demandé. Ils m'ont indiqué un superbe coffret à parfums en ébène incrusté d'or et d'ivoire et portant le nom de la princesse. « Nous avons accepté le coffret, mais j'ai laissé sa bague à la défunte », m'a dit le maître embaumeur. Il m'a alors permis d'examiner la dépouille. Rien qu'au

masque peint d'après les traits de l'infortunée au cours des premières heures suivant son trépas, j'ai compris que la servante
disait vrai : la fille était le portrait craché de sa mère, Néfertiti, que
j'avais vue aux côtés de son époux, aux cérémonies d'Akhet-
Aton. La bague ornée d'un disque d'or sculpté était sans conteste
un bijou royal.

— Mais le père ? demanda Séthi.

Khouper Ptah prit son temps pour répondre.

— La servante m'a confié qu'il était un lieutenant des Écuries
royales, en poste à Hetkaptah, Horamès. Quand l'enfant est né,
il était parti depuis six mois pour Ouaset.

— Personne ne lui aurait dit qu'il avait engendré un prince ?
demanda Séthi.

— Ici, pas à ma connaissance, répondit Khouper Ptah. Nul,
exalté vizir, ne s'y serait risqué. Associé à une princesse et père
d'un prince, il serait en droit de revendiquer je ne sais quel rang
dans le pouvoir. Seul un intrigant, ou un étourdi, se risquerait à
de telles révélations.

— Le père n'a jamais vu le fils ?

— Jamais, à ma connaissance. Ptahmose passe ses journées
avec les scribes et dort avec eux dans l'enceinte du temple.

Séthi hocha la tête. Pa-Ramessou connaissait son père : une
certaine moue de la bouche signifiait qu'il n'était pas entièrement
convaincu par ce qu'il entendait.

— La nourrice n'est jamais venue revoir le garçon qu'elle vous
avait confié ?

— Si, deux ou trois fois, mais nous l'avons éconduite.

L'expression dédaigneuse de Séthi indiqua qu'il n'était toujours pas satisfait. Pourquoi ? se demanda Pa-Ramessou. Il scruta
les expressions du grand-prêtre et du gouverneur : les deux
bonshommes avaient l'air compassés, pas vraiment francs du
collier.

— Et le garçon ? demanda Séthi en coulant un regard vers
son fils.

Car il comprenait que Pa-Ramessou avait, le premier, saisi la
situation : comme celui-ci l'avait craint, Ptahmose pourrait être,
en effet, un prétendant au trône.

— Sa mère ne l'avait pas nommé. Je l'ai appelé Ptahmose et
l'ai élevé comme un de mes enfants. Il apprend maintenant à

écrire. Ni ma femme ni moi n'avons soufflé mot à quiconque de ses origines, et certainement pas à l'enfant.

— Mais beaucoup de gens le savent à Ouaset, déclara Pa-Ramessou, osant prendre la parole pour la première fois.

Khouper Ptah ouvrit de grands yeux, surpris par cette sortie. Ou bien ne disait-il pas la vérité, ou bien ne savait-il pas tout.

— Et moi, ici, à Hetkaptah, je le sais, renchérit le gouverneur.

— J'en suis informé, soupira Khouper Ptah. La servante a beaucoup bavardé. Elle prétend qu'on a rejeté ses demandes de pension et elle est aigrie.

— Il est trop tard pour la faire taire, conclut Séthi. Est-il certain que le garçon ignore le secret de sa naissance?

— Oui, répondit Khouper Ptah. Les ragots de la servante ne peuvent pas être parvenus jusqu'au cercle des scribes.

Le grand-prêtre donna un ordre à l'un des scribes.

Quelques instants plus tard, un garçonnet apparut dans la salle, l'air intimidé et farouche.

6

La volonté de pouvoir

Mince, mais non chétif, les yeux ourlés de cils tellement épais qu'ils paraissaient fardés à l'antimoine, son regard parcourut l'assemblée et s'attarda sur Pa-Ramessou. Il se demandait sans doute lequel des visiteurs avait requis sa comparution, et la présence d'un garçon de son âge l'intriguait particulièrement. La mèche de jeunesse était sagement fixée à la perruque, sur l'oreille droite, mais les orteils frémissaient dans les sandales de cuir ordinaire, et la petite poitrine se soulevait à un rythme plus rapide que la normale.

— Approche, Ptahmose, dit Khouper Ptah, tu as une grande chance et un grand honneur en ce jour. L'illustre vizir du Pays de Horus, Séthi, fils de notre divin roi Ramsès, nous a fait la bonté de nous rendre visite. Salue-le comme il convient à son rang.

Ptahmose avança d'un pas vers la personne que lui désignait le grand-prêtre et s'inclina jusqu'à ce que son front touchât terre. Séthi voulut faire un geste pour interrompre cette prosternation, prématurée chez un garçon de cet âge, mais se ravisa.

— Salut, exalté vizir, déclama le garçon en se relevant. Que la lumière de Rê éclaire tes pas et les mène vers nous, puisque tu la répands autour de toi.

Après avoir récité la formule, il considéra Séthi d'un œil interrogateur. Celui-ci tendit la main et caressa la joue du garçon.

— Salue maintenant le gouverneur, ordonna Khouper Ptah.

Et la cérémonie recommença, mais la prosternation fut limitée à une génuflexion.

— Salue le fils du vizir.

Après une brève hésitation, Ptahmose s'inclina simplement devant le jeune visiteur.

— Salut, noble visiteur. Je loue Ptah d'avoir conduit tes pas vers sa céleste demeure, où je suis à son service.

Les yeux de Pa-Ramessou ne cillèrent pas ; il ne les avait pas détachés de Ptahmose, tentant de déchiffrer quels signes la récitation consciencieuse des formules pouvait dissimuler, mais en vain. Aucune chaleur, aucune curiosité n'avait percé la froide carapace des salutations. Pas un sourire n'avait illuminé son visage. Pour le jeune scribe, ces étrangers n'étaient que cela, des étrangers. Il était clos dans son monde.

Séthi hocha la tête ; ce geste signifiait qu'ils prenaient congé. Il remercia Khouper Ptah et reprit le chemin du Palais ; là, ce fut le gouverneur qu'il remercia et il reprit le bateau pour Ouaset avec son escorte.

— Es-tu satisfait ? demanda-t-il à Pa-Ramessou. Ptahmose ne peut être un rival pour toi.

— Il l'est quand même puisqu'il existe.

La phrase frappa Séthi par sa concision.

— Les ragots de la nourrice ont beaucoup circulé, ajouta Pa-Ramessou. Et je te l'assure, père, Ptahmose sait qui il est.

Ce garçon était décidément précoce. Et singulièrement conscient de ses privilèges.

— Assieds-toi sur mes genoux, dit-il.

Et quand Pa-Ramessou se fut exécuté, le père lui caressa la nuque. Pa-Ramessou enleva sa perruque.

— Tu n'avais pas l'air convaincu par ce que tu as entendu, lança-t-il.

— Tu es fin comme le moustique, convint Séthi. Non, il y avait un point douteux : je ne crois pas que la servante se soit laissé éconduire aussi facilement que le prétend Khouper Ptah. Aucune nourrice ne renoncerait aisément au garçon qu'elle a nourri, surtout s'il s'agit d'un garçon royal. Elle a dû revenir maintes fois jusqu'à ce qu'elle ait obtenu la permission de le revoir.

— Donc Khouper Ptah a menti.

Séthi ne releva pas l'énormité de l'accusation : aller dire qu'un grand-prêtre avait menti, comme un domestique indélicat, cela passait les bornes de la bienséance.

— Nous allons voir ce qu'en pense mon divin père, conclut Séthi.

Ces mots signifiaient que l'affaire ne faisait que commencer. Pa-Ramessou regarda les voiles gonflées de vent, puis il écouta les ahans des rameurs qui, sous le pont, labouraient le Grand Fleuve parce qu'ils étaient nés dans les souterrains de l'espèce humaine et que, là plus qu'ailleurs, la fatalité règne et les avait destinés à cette fonction. Le vent était le caprice des dieux, la rame, le symbole de la sujétion humaine.

Mais Pa-Ramessou ne savait pas encore ces choses-là.

Au dîner, la princesse mère Thouy fut informée des résultats du voyage à Hetkaptah.

— L'histoire est incomplète, déclara-t-elle.

Interloqué, son époux l'interrogea du regard.

— Le grand-prêtre Khouper Ptah prétend que la nourrice n'a jamais revu le garçon, s'écria-t-elle, mais il la laisse caqueter tant et si fort que même Pa-Ramessou perçoit les échos de ses récits à Ouaset. Et il raconte que le garçon Ptahmose ne serait pas informé du secret de sa naissance ? Il prend les gens pour des idiots ?

Séthi fit une grimace ; il ne s'était pas laissé vraiment berner, mais il avait été trop amène avec Khouper Ptah. Réflexion faite, toutefois, il se félicita de ne pas avoir éveillé la méfiance.

— Je l'ai bien dit à mon père chéri, dit alors Pa-Ramessou. Khouper Ptah est un menteur.

L'accusation scandalisa Pa-Semossou et fit pouffer Thiyi.

— Il l'a dit, en effet, convint Séthi.

— Il a essayé de vous endormir, pour que tu n'exiges pas de prendre la garde de ce petit prince, reprit Thouy. Amon seul sait ce qu'il mijote et quel usage il compte en faire plus tard. Et il est bien content des radotages de la nourrice, parce qu'ils répandent le bruit qu'il existe un petit prince à la garde du temple de Ptah.

Pa-Semossou semblait égaré par l'évocation de ces calculs et de ces intrigues autant que par la révélation de l'existence d'un prince de l'ancienne dynastie.

— Mais pourquoi faut-il attribuer tant d'importance à ce garçon ? demanda-t-il.

— Parce qu'il est un instrument dans la main des prêtres, répondit Séthi.

— Les prêtres sont donc nos ennemis ?

— Ils peuvent l'être quand nous faiblissons.

— Séthi, mon maître, il faut agir et rapidement, déclara Thouy.

Le vizir écouta sa femme, se demandant incidemment lequel des deux commandait l'autre.

— D'abord, fais venir la nourrice à Ouaset. Elle sera tout à fait en sécurité dans l'enceinte du palais des Concubines. J'y veillerai.

Séthi hocha la tête. La nourrice était, en effet, à l'origine des rumeurs envahissantes, et il faisait entièrement confiance aux talents de son épouse pour brider le caquet de la matrone.

— Ensuite, fais venir l'enfant.

— Ils ne se le laisseront pas arracher.

— Oseraient-ils résister à l'autorité de ton divin père ? lança-t-elle.

C'était un défi ; il se garda de le relever.

— Je vais voir avec lui.

Ramener Ptahmose à Ouaset ? s'inquiéta Pa-Ramessou. Pour quoi faire ? Mais il était contraint de se rendre à l'évidence : c'était lui qui avait insisté pour clarifier les choses et il serait mal venu d'y trouver à redire. Ptahmose aux mains des prêtres était une menace et la première mesure nécessaire pour le neutraliser était, en effet, de le placer sous le contrôle du Palais.

⚘

Trois jours plus tard, vers dix heures, un certain remue-ménage se fit au palais princier. La princesse Thouy fut prévenue par le directeur des Secrets du matin que « la femme » était arrivée, et elle s'empressa de descendre dans l'un des bureaux du vizir. Pa-Ramessou lui emboîta le pas, suivi de sa sœur Thiyi et de Pa-Semossou.

La femme, à l'évidence, était la nourrice de Ptahmose, et au fur et à mesure que Thouy approchait de la salle indiquée, une autre évidence s'imposait : la nourrice n'était pas venue de son plein gré, loin s'en fallait.

Quand Thouy et ses enfants pénétrèrent dans la salle, une quinquagénaire encore vigoureuse tempêtait en présence de quatre hommes et du deuxième scribe : elle avait, clamait-elle, été enlevée comme une ennemie en temps de guerre et elle s'en plaindrait au pharaon. Mais à la vue de Thouy, elle suspendit ses imprécations. Elle avait deviné qu'elle se trouvait en présence d'une femme d'importance et le Premier scribe le lui confirma en ces termes et d'un ton comminatoire :

— Lève-toi et salue comme il convient l'auguste épouse du noble vizir Séthi.

Les signes de la colère, théâtrale autant que réelle, mais encore plus théâtrale d'être sincère, désertèrent son visage massif, bien qu'affaissé aux mâchoires. Elle dévisagea Thouy, puis son regard se promena de Thiyi à Pa-Semossou et Pa-Ramessou, et revint enfin à Thouy. Comme toutes les servantes de tous les temps et de tous les pays, elle reconnut le pouvoir, dont elle venait d'expérimenter l'efficacité. Le Premier scribe fit avancer des sièges pour Thouy et ses enfants, qui s'assirent, cependant qu'elle, servante de la dernière princesse d'une dynastie déchue dans l'opprobre général, restait debout.

— Comment t'appelles-tu ? demanda Thouy.

— Neser Aton, pour te servir, maîtresse.

« Flamme d'Aton », c'était un nom qui ne correspondait pas à son âge ; il avait dû être ajouté quand la manie monolâtre d'Akhenaton avait imposé le nom du disque solaire à tous ceux de sa cour et du voisinage.

— Ton vrai nom, dit Thouy, avec le calme de l'autorité.

— Je m'appelais jadis Neser Moût, répondit-elle à regret.

« Flamme de la déesse Mère », c'était un nom plus vraisemblable. La nourrice devait être originaire des environs de Karnak, où Moût faisait l'objet d'un culte particulier. Pa-Ramessou, lui, observait les mains de la femme : de vraies griffes de rapace.

— Divine maîtresse, que signifie ce rapt ? reprit la commère. Quatre hommes arrivent à ma maison et me signifient que, sur ordre du vizir, je dois être transférée à Ouaset, ils entassent mes affaires dans un panier et m'entraînent vers un bateau sans me donner le temps de saluer mes amis…

— Demandes-en la raison à ta langue, femme, répondit Thouy. Voilà cinq ans que tu te répands en propos séditieux sur l'existence d'un prince qui devrait être, selon toi, le maître du Pays de Horus, alors que ce pays est béni par le règne du dieu incarné Ramsès…

— Mais ce prince existe ! interrompit l'autre. Le vizir ne l'a-t-il pas de ses yeux vu ?

L'information avait circulé bien vite, à Hetkaptah. Étaient-ce les prêtres qui avaient informé Neser Moût ? Ou bien le jeune Ptahmose lui-même ? En tout cas, la complicité entre la nourrice et le temple était prouvée.

— L'existence de ce garçon n'est pas un motif à bavardages inconsidérés, laissa tomber Thouy.

— Quels bavardages ? glapit Neser Moût. Ma divine maîtresse est morte dans l'indigence, son fils en était réduit à subsister de la charité des prêtres et, moi, je quémandais sur les marchés.

— Sois donc satisfaite. La situation est réglée. Ta demeure est désormais dans ces murs. Le silence sera ton meilleur allié.

Neser Moût comprit la sentence : elle était assignée à résidence et priée de clore son bec.

— Et Ptahmose ? s'écria-t-elle. Que deviendra le rejeton des dieux ?

— Nous aviserons, répondit Thouy. Conduisez cette femme à ses quartiers, au palais des Concubines, ordonna-t-elle en se levant.

Pa-Ramessou, lui, se demandait combien de temps s'écoulerait avant que la nourrice et Horamès ne prissent langue.

La question de Ptahmose n'était toujours pas réglée. Mais comment diable la réglerait-on ?

☙

Plus de deux mois s'étaient écoulés depuis le couronnement de Ramsès Menpehtyrê. La gigantesque machine de l'administration royale se remit alors en route, avec l'efficacité restaurée depuis Horemheb. Après avoir appris les prémices de ces opérations, la famille de Séthi fut informée chaque soir de leurs détails, à l'extérieur et à l'intérieur. Hors des frontières, l'armée fut chargée de faire entendre raison aux populations turbulentes qui avaient sans doute cru que la mort du précédent pharaon leur laissait licence de se rebeller, de piller à qui mieux mieux et de s'abstenir de payer leurs redevances à la couronne, tous ces gens du Kharou, du Djahy, d'Oupi et du Fenkhou[1] de l'est et de l'ouest, sans parler des Tjéhénous, des Shardanes[2], des Shasous, des Apirous et des peuplades de Koush. Quelques expéditions militaires leur feraient entendre raison.

Séthi commença d'ailleurs à s'absenter pour des périodes de plusieurs jours, afin de veiller à la démolition ou à l'occupation de places fortes que ces impertinents s'étaient crus autorisés à construire.

— Quand tu auras atteint l'âge de sagesse, déclara-t-il à Pa-Semossou, je t'emmènerai avec moi. Nous verrons si tu es aussi bon archer que le disent tes maîtres.

Quant à Pa-Ramessou, il lui faudrait encore attendre cinq ans pour avoir droit aux honneurs de la guerre.

À l'intérieur, Ramsès avait fixé à son fils deux objectifs ; le premier consistait à prévenir la reconstitution des milices privées, grâce auxquelles les seigneurs provinciaux avaient cru pouvoir s'affranchir de la tutelle royale sous le règne d'Amenhotep le Quatrième, celui qui s'était fait appeler Akhenaton. Le second objectif était d'amplifier le temple d'Amon à Karnak, pour bien signifier au clergé que l'ordre éternel avait été rétabli et que tout soutien aux seigneurs de province serait particulièrement inopportun. Les deux objectifs étaient liés et, dans le cas où certains gouverneurs auraient témoigné de complaisances à l'égard de potentats du cru, rien ne valait la complicité des prêtres et de leurs scribes pour les dénoncer. Ces gens-là, en effet, étaient le plus souvent de mèche avec les magiciens et les comptables des gros propriétaires, et il n'était en fin de compte d'intrigues mineures qui ne parvinssent à la connaissance des clergés de

---

1. Kharou, Djahy et Oupi désignent des provinces qui correspondent à peu près au nord de la Palestine et au sud de la Syrie. Le Fenkhou est la Phénicie, c'est-à-dire la côte de la Palestine.
2. Peuple de navigateurs originaire d'Asie Mineure ; il finit par se replier sur la Sardaigne, d'où le nom de cette île.

grands et petits temples, querelles d'héritages ou rivalités de marchands, aussi bien que les grands délits, vols ou meurtres.

N'ayant plus guère l'occasion de s'entretenir avec son père, Pa-Ramessou s'en ouvrit à sa mère, un matin dans les appartements de celle-ci. Thiyi, dans la garde-robe voisine, discutait d'un certain plissé avec la faiseuse. La brise filtrait de la terrasse, enflant les draperies et dissipant les dernières traces de parfums qui se consumaient dans le brasero. Le champ était libre. Pa-Ramessou pouvait aborder le sujet.

— Et qu'advient-il de Ptahmose ? demanda-t-il à sa mère, sur un ton pathétique.

— En quoi le sort de ce garçon t'importe-t-il ?

— Mère, s'il faisait valoir ses droits, il me supplanterait !

— Il ne peut les faire valoir sans l'assentiment de ton divin grand-père. Et il est bien tôt, il me semble, répondit Thouy avec un sourire d'ironie, pour songer à tes droits.

— Mais pourquoi ne me dis-tu pas ce qu'il en est ?

Thouy soupira.

— Ton grand-père a demandé aux prêtres de remettre la garde du garçon à ton père. Le grand-prêtre Khouper Ptah a répondu qu'il s'était attaché à lui comme à l'un de ses propres fils et qu'il ne pouvait se soustraire de gaîté de cœur à l'engagement qu'il avait pris de l'élever. Seul le vrai père, a-t-il prétexté, pourrait revendiquer la garde de Ptahmose, mais comme c'est un militaire dont la vie est constamment en danger, il exposerait ainsi le garçon à être une fois de plus orphelin. Voilà, tu vois, c'est une affaire compliquée et ni toi, ni ton père, ni moi ne saurions mieux faire que le pharaon.

Pa-Ramessou se rembrunit. Ce mystérieux rival qu'il n'avait qu'entrevu à Hetkaptah prenait les dimensions d'un monstre.

— Mais alors, mère, ce garçon doit être important, puisque le grand-prêtre résiste même au pharaon ?

— Tu es bien jeune pour t'occuper de ces choses, observa Thouy avec une pointe d'étonnement, sinon d'admiration.

Une servante entra pour regarnir en parfums le brasero.

— Écoute-moi, essaie de comprendre : si nous donnons aux prêtres l'impression que nous accordons de l'importance à Ptahmose, ils lui en attribueront une qui sera encore plus grande.

— Mais qu'est-ce que veulent les prêtres, à la fin ?

— Le pouvoir, comme tous les hommes, Pa-Ramessou. Comme toi. Ils se servent de Ptahmose pour faire pression sur ton grand-père.

— Je suis sûr qu'ils veulent faire de lui un futur pharaon.

— Nous avons le temps de voir venir. Ce n'est pas demain la veille, répondit Thouy en caressant l'épaule de son fils. Pour le moment, ils essaient d'obtenir des avantages comparables à ceux des prêtres d'Amon.

Ce n'étaient pas de telles considérations qui auraient dissipé l'inquiétude et la frustration de Pa-Ramessou. Il l'avait bien pressenti, la situation qui fermentait autour de Ptahmose était dangereuse. Elle menaçait son pouvoir. Oui, son pouvoir.

Mais il ne se laisserait pas faire. Non, pas lui. Sa mère fut appelée à la garde-robe pour une question de repassage des plissés ; il demeura seul, pensif, et sortit sur la terrasse contempler le Grand Fleuve et les barques qui glissaient nonchalamment comme des cornes effilées.

Il trouverait un moyen d'agir. Comment ? Il l'ignorait.

7

Un message clandestin

La faiblesse de l'âge tendre est sa force : c'est l'ignorance du temps et des caprices des dieux.

Pendant les fêtes de l'Inondation, Pa-Semossou tomba malade. Qu'avait-il mangé de corrompu à l'un des banquets de village où il avait accompagné son père ? On l'ignorait. Ni Séthi ni Pa-Ramessou n'avaient été incommodés, mais Pa-Semossou, lui, dut s'aliter. Ses entrailles se vidèrent de façon irrépressible par le haut et par le bas. L'argile et autres remèdes prescrits par le médecin royal furent inopérants. En deux jours de fièvre ardente, son corps rejeta toute son eau et il s'émacia. Le troisième jour, son cœur cessa de battre. Le jeune archer ne lancerait plus ses flèches que vers les étoiles. L'événement affecta le Palais tout entier, à commencer par le dieu incarné Ramsès, dont la mine accablée ne disait que trop la sincérité de son chagrin. Il n'est pas de bon augure qu'un petit-fils s'en aille avant son aïeul.

Sa première expérience de la mort laissa Pa-Ramessou dans la stupeur. Était-ce parce qu'il était un garçon ou bien trop jeune ? Il l'ignorait, mais il n'avait pas le don des larmes, qui permettait à sa mère, à sa sœur et à sa grand-mère de se défaire de leur trop-plein de chagrin. D'ailleurs, ce n'était pas tant la privation qui l'éprouvait, son affection pour son frère ayant été modérée, que la soudaineté du départ et l'offense à son orgueil. Comment, en trois jours, un être humain s'étiolait, puis s'éteignait et sa dépouille était livrée aux embaumeurs ? Cela n'avait pas de sens, c'était insultant ! Cela équivalait à dire aux vivants qu'ils n'étaient, eux aussi, que des fétus de paille. L'incrédulité de Pa-Ramessou ne le céda qu'à l'indignation. Les dernières musiques de la fête s'étaient tues depuis six semaines quand le cortège fluvial qui accompagnait Pa-Semossou au Champ de Maât quitta donc les quais de Ouaset dans les cris des pleureuses.

Pa-Ramessou était dévasté. Il était cependant bien loin d'imaginer les conséquences de l'événement.

Au premier repas du soir qui suivit le retour de la famille au Palais, il éprouva un nouveau choc. Séthi se présenta accompagné de Ptahmose. Ptahmose, oui.

Thouy n'était pas dans le secret, car elle fit des yeux ronds.

— Femme, voici notre nouveau fils. Enfants, voici votre nouveau frère. Les ordres de mon divin père sont accomplis.

La référence aux ordres royaux interdisait aux convives la moindre contestation ou mauvaise grâce, et la présence du garçon excluait également toute interrogation sur les motifs de Ramsès. Ptahmose lui-même semblait effrayé par la soudaineté de cette adoption. Il balbutia des formules de soumission et d'affection à ses nouveaux parents et d'affection tout court à Thiyi et Pa-Ramessou, puis s'enfonça dans un mutisme noir comme le naphte. Séthi lui témoigna tous les signes d'une bienveillance sincère et, par compassion pour un gamin qui venait d'être arraché à son milieu autant que par déférence à l'égard de la volonté du pharaon, Thouy se joignit au jeu ; elle remplit elle-même le plat du nouveau venu et l'engagea à manger, accompagnant ses mots d'un sourire. Même Thiyi se montra enjouée. Pa-Ramessou, lui, était confondu. Le rival devenait donc son frère ? Son frère ? Il ne parvenait pas à détacher ses yeux du jeune prince, mais celui-ci ne lui accorda que deux ou trois coups d'œil à la dérobée.

Tout cela paraissait irréel. Même les domestiques semblaient conscients de l'étrangeté de la situation ; ils avaient eux aussi entendu l'adresse de Séthi arrivant avec le garçon. Nul doute que les bavardages iraient bon train à l'office.

Le souper s'acheva sans que la gêne qui pesait sur les convives se fût levée.

— Ptahmose t'accompagnera demain à l'école, déclara Séthi à Pa-Ramessou.

Sur quoi il donna l'ordre aux domestiques de mener le garçon à ses nouveaux appartements. Nouvelle surprise de Pa-Ramessou : ce seraient ceux du défunt Pa-Semossou. Ptahmose souhaita la bonne nuit à ses nouveaux parents et suivit le maître de la Garde-robe. Ce fut alors que Séthi fit un signe aux siens ; ils le suivirent dans son bureau.

— Hier, dit-il, mon divin père a envoyé deux lieutenants de sa garde à Hetkaptah avec l'ordre écrit de ramener Ptahmose à Ouaset, étant donné qu'il détient l'autorité suprême sur tous les sujets d'ascendance royale et que Ptahmose n'a aucun lien de parenté avec le grand-prêtre de Ptah qui l'a généreusement accueilli. Le grand-prêtre a tenté de tergiverser, mais il a préféré cette fois déférer à la volonté royale et éviter un conflit ouvert.

— Tu n'étais pas informé de son projet ? demanda Thouy.

— Il m'a prévenu sitôt après que ses émissaires sont partis pour Hetkaptah. Il m'a déclaré que nous avions assez discuté avec le clergé au sujet de ce garçon et qu'il ne voyait pas de raison de lui céder la tutelle d'un prince du sang. Il m'a dit : « Tu l'accueilleras dans ta famille comme s'il était votre fils. J'y compte. »

— Comment expliques-tu cette décision ?

— Il a été très affecté par la mort de Pa-Semossou. Il a songé à sa descendance. Il n'a pas oublié la contrariété de Horemheb, qui était mort sans enfants. Il ne lui restait plus qu'un seul petit-fils et il s'est dit que, s'il m'advenait quelque chose de malheureux, les prêtres de Hetkaptah seraient tentés de mettre sur le trône un garçon qu'ils auraient formé et qui serait donc sous leur sujétion.

— Et moi ? s'écria Pa-Ramessou.

— Tu es plus en sécurité avec Ptahmose parmi nous que s'il était encore à Hetkaptah. Quant à l'avenir, ne t'en inquiète pas trop tôt.

— Mais ce garçon n'est pas mon frère !

— Eh bien, fais en sorte qu'il se sente en confiance comme s'il l'était. Songe que son sort est bien triste. Sa mère est morte et son père ne s'est apparemment jamais occupé de lui. Il a été confié aux prêtres de Hetkaptah et, bien que ce ne soient pas en eux-mêmes de mauvaises gens, je ne suis pas sûr que son enfance ait été très heureuse parmi eux. Tu obtiendras davantage par la douceur que par la méfiance.

Pa-Ramessou médita le conseil, mais n'en sembla pas enthousiasmé. Sur quoi Thouy et Thiyi allèrent rejoindre les dames de la cour, comme elles le faisaient le plus souvent après le dîner, et Séthi rejoignit son petit cercle d'intimes pour jouer au *senet*[1] en sirotant du vin cuit aux épices. Peut-être y apprenait-il la ruse.

En passant devant la chambre de son nouveau frère, Pa-Ramessou s'arrêta et, incapable de résister à la curiosité, écarta la draperie et jeta un coup d'œil à l'intérieur. Une veilleuse éclairait la pièce. Le lit était vide. Pa-Ramessou explora les parages du regard. À la fin, il distingua une silhouette sur la terrasse et décida de la rejoindre.

Ptahmose était penché à la balustrade. Que regardait-il? La nuit était sans lune et l'on ne distinguait çà et là que les lumignons des rares bateaux qui passaient. Guère de quoi tenir son garçon éveillé. Ptahmose tourna la tête vers son visiteur.

— Tu n'as pas sommeil? demanda Pa-Ramessou.

— Là-bas, à Hetkaptah, je ne dormais jamais seul, consentit enfin à répondre Ptahmose. Je partageais le lit avec mes frères scribes. C'est effrayant de dormir seul.

— Tu as peur?

— Non, je me sens abandonné.

— Mais nous sommes là…

— Je ne connais pas ta famille et je ne vous ai vus qu'une fois, ton père et toi. Je ne sais pas pourquoi on m'a fait venir ici.

Pa-Ramessou fut troublé par la détresse du garçon, et plus encore par le fait qu'il en était ému, alors qu'une heure auparavant, il considérait Ptahmose comme un intrus.

— Tu veux dormir avec moi?

Un silence passa.

— Oui, je préfère.

— Alors allons-y, j'ai sommeil.

Ils se défirent de leurs perruques, de leurs pagnes et de leurs sandales et s'allongèrent.

— Tu es roux? demanda Ptahmose, comme s'il doutait de ce qu'il avait vu.

— Ne suis-je pas le fils de Seth?

---

1. Jeu comparable au jacquet et aux dames, qui devint en vogue sous le Nouvel Empire.

La réponse déconcerta probablement Ptahmose car il demeura muet. Au bout d'un moment, il se blottit contre son frère de circonstance, ignorant que ce dernier l'avait exécré pendant des mois. Pa-Ramessou, lui, recru d'émotions contradictoires et las de penser, s'était déjà endormi sur sa repartie. À l'aube, il se leva pour pisser et regagna sa chambre.

Au petit déjeuner, il lui sembla que Ptahmose s'était adouci et même qu'il lui avait adressé un petit sourire. Il ne sut plus ce qu'il en était de ses propres craintes. Une seule nuit partagée avait-elle donc suffi à métamorphoser un rival en un quasi-frère? Il remâchait encore sa perplexité quand Ptahmose et lui se mirent ensemble en route pour le *kep*. Derechef il observa l'autre à la dérobée, guettant Amon seul savait quel signe de la vilenie foncière de celui qu'il avait, jusqu'à son arrivée au Palais, tenu pour un rival. En vain.

Le soir venu, Ptahmose bredouilla :

— Tu ne me laisserais pas dormir seul ce soir?

— Non.

À la fin, songea Pa-Ramessou, Ptahmose pourrait bien prendre une place plus grande que celle du défunt Pa-Semossou. L'imprévisible glissement de la haine à un sentiment qui ressemblait à une véritable affection fraternelle s'exerçait d'autant plus facilement que Pa-Ramessou détenait le beau rôle dans cette adoption inattendue. N'était-ce pas grâce à sa générosité que Ptahmose s'acclimatait à son nouveau milieu familial? De surcroît, il n'avait jamais exercé d'emprise sur Pa-Semossou, son aîné, alors qu'il dominait déjà le nouveau venu, à qui il servait de guide et de conseiller.

La preuve en fut que, le troisième soir, il enjoignit à Ptahmose de venir dormir dans sa chambre, c'est-à-dire dans son territoire.

Entre-temps, les gens de la Garde-robe s'étaient avisés que les gamins partageaient le même lit et, sur l'assentiment de Séthi, ils disposèrent un grand lit dans la chambre de Pa-Ramessou.

Le rival était devenu un sujet, si ce n'est un féal.

Cependant, guère enclin à partager la sieste avec Ptahmose, Pa-Ramessou avait repris ses excursions dans les entrailles des palais. Bien lui en prit, du moins le pensa-t-il.

Le premier jour, il se retrouva dans les sous-sols du palais des Concubines. Situé à l'opposé des quartiers de la garde et des écuries, le bâtiment lui avait toujours paru mystérieux et frappé d'inutilité. Bien qu'il ne sût pas grand-chose des femmes et à peine plus de l'administration des palais, son instinct ne l'avait qu'à peine trompé. Réservé en principe aux favorites du pharaon et des princes, le palais des Concubines servait aussi d'auberge aux chanteuses et danseuses de la cour, sous la juridiction des matrones alliées aux mères, belles-mères et sœurs des dignitaires, qui eussent encombré, voire importuné les couples dans leurs appartements de fonction.

Dans sa malveillance pointue à l'égard du monde des adultes, commune aux enfants, Pa-Ramessou ignorait cependant que le palais des Concubines était bien cela : le seul domaine du Pays de Horus où les femmes régnaient sans partage. Les occupantes de cette enclave traditionnelle y échappaient au pouvoir et aux lubies des mâles, engeance fragile autant que brutale, qui n'émergeait des naïvetés de l'adolescence que pour saccager le monde, puis choir dans les radotages désabusés de la sénilité.

La raison d'être officielle du palais des Concubines était d'héberger une douzaine et demie de donzelles en âge de procréer. Théoriquement destinées à fournir la dynastie en rejetons, de préférence mâles, elles se tenaient, nuit et jour, lavées et parfumées, à disposition du dieu incarné, au cas où sa Première Épouse se trouvât incommodée ou, plus prosaïquement, il aurait désiré changer d'ordinaire. À vrai dire, elles se languissaient d'ennui ; depuis des lustres, les monarques ne les visitaient que rarement. Toutankhamon, par exemple, ne semblait pas avoir éprouvé ces chaleurs des reins, pourtant ordinaires à son âge, qui poussent les hommes à se reproduire, fût-ce en dehors des liens supposés du couple ; aussi n'avait-il pas eu de descendance. Son successeur Aÿ avait sans doute été trop vieux pour se livrer à des exploits sexuels surnuméraires et le palais des Concubines n'avait guère résonné de ses pas. Passait encore.

Dans les campagnes, où l'on pratiquait un robuste bon sens, il se disait que la paresse du pénis était causée par un excès d'unions consanguines dans la lignée. Trop d'enfants royaux étaient nés d'un frère et de sa sœur, quand ce n'était pas d'un père et de sa fille, et on les reconnaissait à une apparence trop délicate, signe d'une nature chétive confirmée par les années ; le premier croup, ou la première varicelle, les emportait. Mais Horemheb, vaillant guerrier de souche plébéienne, ne s'était pas non plus illustré par sa fougue auprès de ses almées. Aucune d'elles n'avait l'ombre d'un souvenir de ses capacités amoureuses, et les anecdotes graveleuses à son sujet se limitaient aux ragots sur le fait qu'il aurait délégué un jeune et beau lieutenant des Écuries à la fécondation de sa Première Épouse, sans résultat comme on savait. Et les donzelles attendaient toujours la visite du nouveau pharaon, Ramsès.

Vingt vierges aux petits seins ronds et aux fesses rebondies, vingt créatures au sexe neuf et rose, et pas de rejetons ! Le dieu Mîn, à qui les sculpteurs et les peintres prêtaient une érection sacrée permanente et phénoménale, ne paraissait vraiment pas avoir comblé les maîtres du pays. Mais l'exactitude incitait à reconnaître que, de surcroît, ceux-ci se méfiaient des concubines : certaines histoires fâcheuses pour leur réputation circulaient, en effet, dans les couloirs du Palais. La plus célèbre était celle d'une concubine qui s'était fait engrosser par un officier de la Bouche – piquante coïncidence – et s'était ensuite vantée d'avoir été fécondée par le dieu vivant. Hélas, le monarque, en l'occurrence Toutankhamon, n'avait pas souvenir d'avoir jamais comblé la pécore. Aussi avait-elle été renvoyée dans ses provinces, sans jamais accéder au rang exalté de Deuxième Épouse royale.

Aussi l'inévitable s'était-il produit : désespérant de jamais recevoir la semence divine, les concubines se donnaient du plaisir entre elles, sous prétexte de s'entraîner à leur métier de donneuses de plaisir. Renonçant même à leur virginité, certaines recouraient à des faux-semblants d'ivoire ; des artisans complaisants leur avaient même confectionné des olisbos doubles, afin qu'elles pussent avoir des émois en couple. Déconcertante parodie où chacune pouvait tenir le rôle de l'amant céleste tout en étant l'aimée terrestre.

Pa-Ramessou n'était évidemment pas censé savoir ces choses, mais si énigmatiques qu'elles fussent, diverses allusions goguenardes de sa mère et de fonctionnaires de la Garde-robe l'avaient déniaisé avant l'heure, intellectuellement tout au moins. Il se représentait le palais des Concubines comme un repaire de dames qui se livraient à des parodies de fornication, autrement dit, comme une boutique de faux-semblants. Sur ce point, cependant, son dédain était mal fondé, sans quoi il n'eût pas eu le loisir d'accéder au bâtiment, fût-ce par les sous-sols. En d'autres temps interdit aux sujets du sexe mâle, en effet, ce palais était devenu une passoire, dans ses profondeurs tout au moins, et l'on n'y prêtait donc pas attention à un gamin fureteur.

Or, c'était dans ce bâtiment qu'était recluse Neser Moût, la nourrice de feu Néferneferourê, mère de Ptahmose. Et Pa-Ramessou avait son idée : en dépit des dénégations de Khouper Ptah, la matrone avait continué à voir le garçon. Elle lui avait certainement révélé son ascendance et, si c'était bien le cas, Ptahmose, en dépit de ses mines éplorées, nourrissait des idées ambitieuses et téméraires quant à son avenir. Mais comment le vérifier ?

Il rôdait depuis un moment. Des esclaves allaient et venaient dans les couloirs éclairés par des lumignons fuligineux ou bien des meurtrières percées au ras du sol, portant des paniers de linge, de petites amphores, des sacs d'objets indistincts. Elles allaient pieds nus sur la terre battue, un pagne de pudeur autour des reins, les seins nus ballottant de droite et de gauche, la tignasse à l'air ou bien quasi tondues, quelques-unes mâchant du *khat*. Grande fut l'émotion de Pa-Ramessou quand, au départ d'un escalier, il surprit l'échange suivant entre deux femmes :

— Où vas-tu ? J'ai besoin de toi ici.

— Je vais chez Neser Moût prendre son linge pour le porter à la buanderie. Ordre de la grande maîtresse.

— C'est pour le linge seulement, ou bien pour porter encore un message au petit prince ?

— Elle me donnera certainement un message, je pense.

La première esclave soupira.

— Fais attention que la grande maîtresse ne t'attrape pas ou, pis encore, le maître. Ils te feraient fouetter.

— Ne t'inquiète pas.

Caché derrière un des piliers des fondations, Pa-Ramessou se garda de quitter son repaire. Quelques instants plus tard, la route était libre. Il revint sur ses pas et gagna un autre escalier menant au grand jardin qui séparait le palais du Grand Fleuve. Il erra un moment entre les palmiers et les rosiers, jusqu'aux berges herbues. Une barque, *Le Bonheur d'Isis*, se balançait à l'extrémité

He turned to Semi with his eyebrows tented. "You're leaving?" The thought hurt him. *Why*? He was going to miss her. She had become more than "formidable." She was his friend. His only friend in Kzhek that he could trust beyond question. She was more than a friend. That thought stung the inside of his mind like a Gruth bay eel. *Is she returning for our people, or to flee the cause?*

She nodded and shifted her gaze to Thane Leisa.

Why is she always so quiet around the nobility?

"Semi, you know you don't have to do everything they tell you. Is this what *you* want or what *they* want?" He checked Thane Leisa's reaction and was relieved to see that she bore a dismissive grin.

"Semi has already prepared to leave tomorrow. Why don't you two take some time to talk this over? You will find a study three doors down to your left."

The walk to the other chamber was as silent as a guilty prisoner on his way to the executioner's block. Tension shifted into curiosity and shame. *Did I embarrass her?* He had to repair his mistakes before she left.

Am I jealous of her freedom? A chance to return to my people? An escape for the epicenter of conflict?

The room proved true to Thane Leisa's description of "comfortable," contrasting the chill of her office with plush couches and a thick rug from a black bear. The aroma of anise and lavender filled the air.

"Semi..."

"No, I'm fine. I understand your concern. I will not deny that they tried to convince me to go, but I chose this task." Her responses accomplished little in resolving the sorrow on his face. "If you're concerned about my doubts..."

"Are you still worried about all of this?"

"Of course I'm worried, but Thane Leisa is an Endowed as well. We had some thorough discussions about the morality of it all. What about you, Yetrik? How do you feel? Happy to stay with Royss. Or are you simply sad to see me leave?"

Images of Royss and the beaten rebel flashed through his mind. He tried to forget it by forcing a smile upon himself.

"I *believe* I'm doing well. My life has been more exciting than it ever was back home. I've plotted defenses with the nobility, hunted kaesan, and I'm sure much more is ahead."

"I'm happy to hear that. I was lost until I said that I would return to Gruth."

"We'll see each other again, right?" he asked.

"Those who fight together are always the closest in the bard's tales!"

"Like Camn and Aoll? The warriors who led their people to victory in the Elder era and celebrated with a suicide pact?"

"What an imperfect example, Yetrik." She smiled.

Hope touched his heart.

She pushed her hair behind her ear. "Maybe I will make it back here before they send you home. Your return will be much better than mine. If you keep helping out here, I'm sure the Krall will want you for one of his Thanes. I can already see it now. Thane..." Her jaw dropped. "I don't think I've ever heard your surname."

"Kloff," said Yetrik, "and yours?"

"Ershif."

"Is that of Zhaes origin? I would gamble that I have met at least one Ershif during our stay."

She extended her palm. "Pay me! Ershif is southern Gruth, more Gruth than Kloff, that sounds Chuss to me."

"Could be," he shrugged, "I never thought to ask my parents."

They looked away from each other.

Semi turned back. "Do you know what Royss is going to have you do while you stay?"

"No idea." *Anything but combat,* he prayed.

"Do you... does Royss make you feel like something is wrong?"

"What do you mean?" He didn't need to ask. He knew exactly how she felt and failed to recognize it until Royss took him to see the protests.

"I feel like he has more plans of his own. Plans that he doesn't share with the Court."

"Thane Gett trusts him. That is enough for me for now."

"Right," she nodded and leaned forward to dive into her thoughts. "Do you think that there is more going on in Facet besides anti-harvesting protests? I feel like this is just a part of something larger that is yet to come."

"I'm sure of it," Yetrik slouched back against the seat. "Thane Gett sends us to Zhaes at the cusp of war and *suddenly* we are accepted among the Zhaes nobility to help plot? Who was to guess that the protests would escalate to where they now stand? I don't fear conspiracy, I just have questions. Simply stated, we see a single drop of the oncoming rainstorm."

She nodded. "How odd."

"What?"

"*War.* They plan to 'silence protests,' but will only invigorate them. How foolish are we to think that we can solve this by showing who has more power."

"I'm sure they have made attempts to find peace with the protesters."

She laughed. "They? Who, the Zhaes Thanes? They're too prideful for that. EVen if they have tried something, it is not enough." She shook her head. "What have we become to resort to resolving conflicts as wild beasts?"

"I... I don't know," Yetrik muttered. He tried to think of some solution to her concern, searching for a justification for combating violence with violence, but he was at a loss of words. "Perhaps discipline is the sole way a parent can correct a rebellious child set on sedition."

"Parents are imperfect beings, given the illusion of authority by age. Everyone is young on the inside. There is no *right* in this conflict, only a contest between less-desirable outcomes."

"I thought you and Thane Leisa were able to talk through your worries?"

"When has anyone completely *overcome* a concern, Yetrik? People learn to bear their burdens before they can dismiss them. I'm still trying to hold mine before I collapse. *Perding under realms.* I thought I came here for a discussion of trade, but now I wonder if I'm the only Endowed poised to oppose the war." She sighed and straightened her posture to return to Yetrik's eyes. "If I cannot prevent, I will do my best to protect by serving my people at home."

"*My people?*" Yetrik lost the grace of a smile, "They're as much *my people* as they are yours."

"Do not forget that, Yetrik Kloff. The Zhaesmen may be persuaded to treat you otherwise."

꙳ꙮ꙳ ꙮ꙳ꙮ

Yetrik was taken back to the Canton of Agriculture by carriage. It was late and would have been safer to sleep at the Canton of Veneration, but he did not want to be another one of Semi's burdens. He feared he had pushed her too far already for one day.

Candles shimmered along the Canton's outer walls, dancing like spirits on polished stone. Two guards stared out into the night on each side of the main door. He suspected that more would be hiding or patrolling the perimeter, helping the Canton remain one of the few protected buildings in the heart of Kzhek.

The guards opened the door without question. He wondered how far his reputation had spread.

The inner chambers were barren, aside from some more guards. One guard offered to guide him, but he declined. Yetrik knew that Royss tended to stay on the second level. Royss was one of the last people that Yetrik wanted to see at that moment, but he knew the Thane would keep him safe for the night. He needed to make the Thane aware of where he was.

Yetrik ascended the extensive staircase in the center of the chamber, avoiding loud movements to not disturb any who slept. That was another odd Zhaes habit that he had noticed. It was not uncommon for a laborer to spend the night in the Canton in which they worked. They claimed it was to allow an individual to work from the very beginning and end of their day. Perhaps that was the origin of Zhaes' harsh and near loveless culture. People became less like fathers and mothers and more underlings and tools for the benefit of the Court.

Hushed banter, with an occasional laugh, emanated from a door near the end of the right hallway. More light shimmered along the floor.

"Yes, and... well... the kulf of a..." it sounded like Royss.

He opened the door to a room that looked like a personal tavern.

"Yetrik!" said Royss."Come quickly and shut the door." Royss stood behind the counter with a bottle of blue wine in his right hand, cork removed as he continued to pour it into a pewter goblet for the man across from him.

The man across from Royss sat on a high stool that looked as if it would soon become a pile of splinters under his weight. He was built like a bronze statue of an ancient warrior, nearly doubling the size of Royss with muscle that denied any hint of fat. His skin stretched over bulging veins. He wore a collared vest of Zhaes gray with bronze lining the middle. Youth glimmered in his face, though a rigid beard, aged his countenance, complimenting his black hair that descended to the base of his neck with shaved sides.

"A Gorger?" Yetrik spilled out. Royss took his reaction with humor, though he held a finger to his mouth to quiet the excitement.

"Is this the Gruthman you spoke of, Royss?" said the Gorger.

"Yes, this is Yetrik." Royss turned to Yetrik. "Yetrik this is Taeih, one of Zhaes' most renowned Gorgers and a distant relative of mine. The cousin of a cousin type of relationship."

Taeih downed some wine, then whipped his mouth. "Pleasure to meet you, Gruthman."

"Likewise," responded Yetrik. "Why are you two still awake?"

"I should ask you the same question," said Royss after a pull on his drink. The blue wine had stained his teeth a dark shade of purple, though neither of them had drunk enough to become inebriated. "I am a Thane and may do as it pleases me, but *you* should rest to prepare for the coming days."

Yetrik dropped the corners of his mouth and searched for an excusing defense.

"I assume you need a room for you and Semi?" Royss chuckled as Yetrik opened his mouth to protest. "You are too easy to rile up. In all seriousness, how was your meeting with her? Were you able to meet with Thane Leisa?"

"Yes, she was very kind. Pleasant and hospitable." A humorous sneer rose in Royss as he described her pleasantries. "Semi and I had a good discussion."

"And...what did you speak about? Is she still opposed to our offense against the protests?"

Yetrik shrugged. He was not going to betray her. He knew she would find confidence in the need to preserve harvesting. "I think her mind is too focused on Court Gruth right now. I suppose you know that she is going back to Thusk."

"I was the one who suggested it."

Yetrik doubted that. "Speaking of Gruth, what about Thane Gett? She is going to be working more with our Thanes. Should we update him on his request for bronze?"

"As you can tell, Gruthman, we have become quite preoccupied as a Court. He should have had that vision months ago. Once the central protests have been cleared and we have a firmer foundation here in Kzhek, we can focus on his request, if it is still relevant."

Taeih turned back and forth to each man as he orated with the interest of a hound to a stick in his owner's hand, though he avoided interjecting.

"Are Semi's worries burdening you?" asked Royss.

"I wouldn't say I'm overburdened, but it is taxing to have my only Gruth ally so shaken. But how was your time with her, Royss?" Yetrik stepped up to sit on the stool beside Taeih.

"She did not want to talk about her concerns. Said she would rather focus on the task at hand and mostly kept to herself. She is a quiet girl, though wise beneath her shell. Her logic is merely flawed by passion and empathy. She wasn't the one who helped us gain the support of the Gorgers. Taeih helped us there." Taeih raised his goblet at his mention, taking another drink.

Yetrik stared at him with puzzled discomfort and shifted his eyes to Royss, who had not touched his drink since he had intruded on their meeting.

Royss smiled. "Gorgers process all foods differently than we do. That includes alcohol."

"I still feel the sting," pitched Taeih mid-drink, "but it is gone within a moment."

"Like Shiftlings? Semi said she processed alcohol in the same way." Yetrik said.

"Shiftlings have to force their digestive manipulation," said Taeih. "We Gorgers do so without a thought and are more efficient. I've never lost a drinking match to a Shiftling."

"That was one piece of conversation that Semi and I could resort to. The girl knows more about drinks than anyone I have met in a tavern."

"I was surprised to learn how well she knew her way around drinks," said Yetrik. "She asked for Middleman's bane in the first tavern on our way here." Taeih coughed on his wine with eyes opened in shock, which inspired a timely laugh from Royss and Yetrik.

"A curious one, that girl. Speaking of *the Middlemen*, she mentioned you had quite an infatuation for them." Royss passed his half-full goblet over to Taeih, who had already finished the bottle on the table. His lips were stained with the cyan coloration of a man hanging from the gallows.

Did I ever mention them to her? Had she read my notes? He could not recall talking to her about them, but was sure he mentioned them in passing. Passionate interests fall from one's mouth like drool from a smiling hound. "She did? It is nothing to worry about. Just some curiosity."

"Can I not be just as curious? If the Chussmen still deal with them, they must have some valuable resources in their land. If no one else cares to search them out, why shouldn't you? Bridge the crevices lost to all but the Chussmen!"

Yetrik laughed with mild embarrassment. Anyone before Royss had dismissed his engrossment as a childish fascination. "Perhaps."

"No need to shy away from your interest. People jest over the kaesan, though they are much more than a frightening tale for disobedient children. The kaesan are going to be a valuable resource for us as we face the dissenters. What could the Middlemen bring?"

"Maybe someday, when I have the time and resources to travel to the Middlelands," said Yetrik. Royss' face grew serious.

"This is no jest Yetrik. The Patriarchy has knowledge of their encampment locations, though that information lies dormant. I am just as interested as you are, but have been shut down in the past. Once Kzhek peace returns to Kzhek, we can talk about a journey to the Middlelands."

"You're serious?" Yetrik asked.

"As serious as a Zhaes priest."

"No one traverses the pass to reach the Middlelands anymore. It's said to be perilous to the most experienced of travelers!"

Royss shrugged his shoulders, "that sounds like an excuse made by the Chussmen to keep us away. I'll mention your interest to Thane Gromm. The Middlemen could be a valuable asset in protecting harvesting if we can bring them to our side."

"Thank... you. Thank you Royss. It means a lot."

"Tis' a small expression of gratitude for your assistance." Yetrik smiled, though he retracted a degree of joy, wondering if Royss was sending him to perish on the road in the infinitesimal chance of retrieving any valuable resource.

"You've finished a ghete's weight in wine already this evening, Taeih. Ready to call it a close?" Taeih took a final pull on his goblet and finished the last drops from the bottle itself by suspending it above his head with a fat tongue falling out of his open mouth. He nodded, the stool cracking as he stood. Royss looked away from the Gorger to Yetrik, who stood with a plea on the edge of open lips. "I assume you need somewhere to sleep?" Yetrik nodded. "I can lead you to a room."

Taeih left for the evening while Royss led Yetrik to a smaller chamber three doors down from the council room. It was not as ornate as the previous room, but it had a divan long enough for him to sleep on.

"Will this do, Gruthman? Materials are in the bottom drawer of the far cupboard if you find yourself in need of a drinking glass or a light for the candles."

"This should do just fine."

"See you in the morning." Yetrik nodded to dismiss Royss as he closed the door with ease behind him. His footsteps drained down the hall and staircase.

Yetrik was encumbered by excitement and apprehension. Semi, despite her humble intentions, had returned to his mind to face the anxieties of war. Aside from fear, he aimed to harness the excitement of Royss' willingness to encourage his journey to the Middlelands. All previous scholars rejected his interest in the Middlemen; a Brother of the Patriarchy seemed to be a much worse audience for his propositions. If Royss suggested it, he would comply. *How far would that trust go? If Semi were to return to Thusk, only to receive a rejection to their alliance, how would Royss deal with him?*

❧❧❧❧❧ ❧❧❧❧❧

Footsteps stomped in the hallway like hail on a tin rooftop. Yetrik blinked to clear his vision. An orange light glowed beneath his doorway. The sun had not yet risen. *Who is marching about in the middle of the night?* He ruffled his hair and walked over to the door, only to have it pulled open before him by one of Royss' underlings'. He closed his eyes to let in the light more gradually.

"What is the matter?" he groaned with a voice not yet awakened.

"We were too late," the girl said, distraught.

"What?" He squinted at her, pupils dilating to the hall's shine.

"They call themselves '*the Harmony Allegiant*.' Royss is being held hostage, and intruders have occupied the Canton!"

Yetrik stared at her with an open mouth and deadened eyes, wondering if he had not yet awoken.

She gripped his shoulders with a shake. "Chuss, Sleff, and Tchoyas have invaded Kzhek!"

CHAPTER TWENTY-FIVE

MOUNT OF THE ALLEGIANT

"Thane Stolk!" shouted Sleffman as he approached the Chuss captain.

"What is your report?"

"The Cantons of Agriculture, Scholarship, and Diplomacy have been captured and are held by at least forty soldiers each."

Their entrance in the city was more successful than Phenmir could have hoped for. The capture was going well enough that he worried they were missing something. The army made it to Kzhek in a few days, with only minor complications. They sent ahead scouting parties to clear the way, taking out any who might alert the city of an invasion. Some Zhaesmen were bound to recognize an invading army, but they traveled as fast as possible to catch the city unprepared. They had already entered some small fights outside of Kzhek, but the battle was yet to come. Once they had arrived in Kzhek, they sent groups of forty to fifty soldiers to seize the unsuspecting Cantons while the other troops remained near the edge of the city.

"Praise Charic. Send word to Port to move on."

"Yes, sir!" They exchanged salutes, and the Sleffman left the chamber.

Phenmir stood atop the outer balcony of the Canton of Utilities, watching the city lights of the city. Allegiant troops were invading the other Zhaes Cantons. They focused on two cantons at a time and moved on to the next after they captured the Canton's respective Thane. With the Cantons under their control, the Allegiant planned to join the central protesters to capture Kzhek before the Zhaes nobility had a chance to react. They were yet to join with the central protests, but Phenmir was confident that they could gain their support with most of the Cantons captured. Only four of the eight Zhaes Cantons had been captured–though only three remained, noting the collapsed Canton of Endowment–but Phenmir held high hopes.

He left the balcony and walked back inside

Five guards stood inside against the wall. They had been in the city for a few hours, much lies ahead of these soldiers. It was only the beginning of a long battle and an even more exhausting war. Victory in Kzhek was only a step towards victory, not the reward itself.

He observed each of the soldiers in the room, thanked them for their diligence, and left to confront the captive Thane of Utilities.

Thane Sentree sat in an aged wooden chair. Her wrists and ankles were bound to her seat with a thick- rope. Pale skin glowed with a flush above and below the wrist bindings.

"I suppose you are the leader of these rebels?" she said, inspecting his armament.

He approached her, though remained paces away in case of an out-burst. The Zhaesmen in this Canton were surprisingly cooperative with their captors.

"One of them, Thane... Sentree? Is it?" she nodded as he pulled a chair to sit beside her. "Well then, I appreciate your compliance."

She laughed. "Do I have a choice?"

"We have to begin somewhere if we ever hope to reach peace."

"Peace? Is that what you call this? Each person shapes their narrative to please them. The tendency of the prideful."

Phenmir wanted to shout back at her, but clenched his fists to contain himself.

"If this city complies with the will of the people, we can avoid excess suffering."

"What people?" she scoffed. "You think those dissenters represent our Court?"

"We know how you wish to deal with them. We hold most of your nobility, only a few more remain to be seated and bound as you are."

"What do you wish to gain in threatening us? Torturing us until we submit to your rule?"

"We want to remain as civil as possible. Cooperate and we don't have to go to such dire ends." *Perd me if we ever have to go so far.* "Call off the attack on the rioters. Give us time to work with them in a more dignified manner. Let us settle the disputes. Violence against them will only provoke our retribution. Please. Prevent suffering on both sides."

She sighed. "I couldn't call this off even if I wanted to. I am only one of the Thanes and have no control over my Court's decision."

"Which of your Thanes is directing this front?"

"I may *understand* your approach, but still disagree with it. I am no traitor. You suggest avoiding violence, but you are the guilty party by bringing an army into our city. Laeih punishes those who disrupt the rightful order of all."

"Cheric punishes those who take life as a thing of naught." *And I am due for such punishment.* He stood to leave.

"Where are you going, Chussman?"

"If you decide to collaborate, my men shall send for me; otherwise, I leave you to your thoughts."

Phenmir passed by the entrance hall of the Canton, but stopped as he noticed a familiar mask standing among soldiers.

"Voln," Phenmir called. The boy walked up to him.

"Yes, Sir-Medic-Sir-Thane-of-Harmony-Captain-of-the-Allegiant-Lord-of-Chuss Stolk!"

Phenmir tried to hold a stern face, but grinned at the Tchoyasboy.

"Can you shift into an animal less conspicuous than a direwolf? Anything that wouldn't scare someone?"

"Why? I can't grow or shrink. If you want a mouse or ghete, you're out of perding luck."

"I need you to relay a message to the other Cantons we have captured."

"Do you want a dog? Putle? Lynx."

"Putle are too much a Tchoyas creature, and frankly more unusual to see in a city than a direwolf. A dog is fine, but make sure it is a breed usually seen in Zhaes."

He morphed before Phenmir's eyes, all jowls and long ears. "How's this?"

Phenmir shook away the discomfort of hearing an animal speak. "No, still too Tchoyas. Zhaes breeds are slender, the kind used for racing."

"Ah," said the dog. He grew nearly twice as tall as the previous breed. An elongated face stared at him with thin gray fur no longer than an eyelash.

"Perfect, follow me. I'm sure we can find a map for you. We can fasten it to you with a small satchel."

Voln returned to his natural form and followed him upstairs.

Phenmir recalled having at least one map with his belongings, using it to plan their initial entrance into the city. If he ever wished to have a squire, now was the time. He looked to Voln, wondering how he would fare as a squire if the war continued on long enough. *No. A boy of such skill shouldn't be confined as a shield-bearer.*

He remembered handing a younger trooper a rucksack, finding it too cumbersome alongside the commander's armor. Phenmir found the trooper on the second floor, the bag still at his side.

"Chussman," he called, "the bag, please?"

"Yes, Thane Stolk!" he said with an overly servile tone, like a boy who feigned a deeper voice on the edge of puberty.

"I only need the map inside." The boy nodded, removing the small scroll from the bag and handing it to Phenmir. "Remind me of your name, Chussman?"

"Sholmir, sir."

"Thank you for your contribution, Sholmir." Phenmir would forget the name within the hour, but figured the boy's respect had earned some recognition.

They returned to the main level and found a small table, upon which Phenmir rolled out the map and oriented himself to their location. He pointed with his right index finger to a small square that depicted the Canton of Utilities. "We are here. See it, Voln?"

The boy stared at the surrounding guards, many of which continued to stare at him with awe following his transformation.

"I need you to deliver a message to these locations to see if we can convince any Zhaes Thane to help prevent the attack on the city center." He pointed to the Cantons of Agriculture, Scholarship, and Diplomacy. "Thane Holmn is holding the Canton of Scholarship, with Thane Trhet in the Canton of Agriculture. Port should have left for the Canton of Diplomacy by now. Do this as quickly as possible." Voln nodded. "Each minute is crucial. This could save lives, Voln. Is this clear?"

"I understand," he replied.

He placed his palm on the boy's shoulder. "I value you more than it might seem." He gave him a firm pat on the back. "Go!"

Phenmir paced about the room. Their initial entrance into the city had gone without repercussions, but he could only see a small glimpse of what was happening in the Court.

❧❧❧❧❧ ❦❦❦❦❦

Someone knocked on the door to the Canton of Utilities with forceful pounding. Guards were startled and turned to the door in defensive stances. The knocks continued with loud slams as if someone were hitting it with their forearm and fist in unison.

Phenmir descended the stairs, walking up to the door without hesitation.

"Thane Stolk, sir," said the startled guard, holding his hand out. "Let us answer the door."

"No Zhaesman would pound on the door like a hungry child locked out of his house." He unlocked the bolts and opened the door to Voln, who was still panting with hands on his knees.

"I went as fast as I could! See? I'm not slow!" he said with a gasp of air.

"I never lost faith." Phenmir invited him in and led him to the Canton's dining hall.

"Did you get lost?" Phenmir poured water into a small goblet for Voln.

"No, why? I wasn't that long, was I?" His breath gradually returned as he sat slouched at the table side.

"No," Phenmir chuckled. "You were quite swift." He sat at the table across from Voln, placing the water with a small plate of dried meat and bread before him. He would have liked to offer the boy a better dish, but they had few choices while trying to invade a city.

Voln did not seem to mind the food, shoving it through his mask with no thought of its appearance.

"How do your people eat, Voln?"

"What do you think? You kulf! Through our perding mouths, like anyone else."

"I know, but… those like Thane Trhet, with masks covering their mouths. How do they eat with a mask that has molded itself to their face?"

"You should know more than me, med." He paused to finish his water. "The mask only binds to certain portions of our faces, some more than others, but the area around the mouth is free to move so we can speak. Some Tchoyasmen can remove the small pieces that cover their mouth for eating and drinking." He used a wet finger to grab the final crumbs from his plate. "Do you have more of this? It tastes like perding dirt, but I'm starving!"

"We can find some more later."

Voln groaned.

Phenmir drank some water from his own glass. "Did you deliver the message and leave or stay to see the Thanes' responses?"

"I stayed. What fun is a war without watching its games?"

"Thank Cheric, I had forgotten to tell you that we would need a response. I should have known you would be curious enough to linger."

"How long was I out there?"

"Anywhere between three to four hours."

Despite the wooden box placed beneath him on his seat, he still found himself looking up at Phenmir's eyes. "Not a single Thane wished to comply."

Phenmir inhaled slowly. "Did you learn anything?"

"A messenger entered the Canton of Diplomacy alongside me. I heard him tell Port that we have captured the Cantons of Progress and Veneration."

"Leaving the Canton of Haleness as our last piece." Phenmir smiled and let out a light laugh. "Seems appropriate for me, does it not? How are the other Cantons holding?"

"Some Zhaesmen are attacking our troops, trying to recapture the Cantons. Some of them were guards, but I saw even more without armor."

"How bad is it?"

"They are fine. We have more soldiers than they do, but more Zhaesmen are joining their side quickly."

"We need to hurry."

"Yes, best hurry and take control!" Voln took a few steps back from the table.

"I doubt the Thane of Haleness will comply. That kulf never gave a thought to my recommendations while I served him. The longer we wait to join the center, the more time they have to prepare their attack on the center."

"What are you suggesting, Chussman?"

Phenmir regained focus on the present and stood to face Voln. "I need you to relay another message to each of the captured Cantons as soon as possible. I will send another messenger by ghete to inform the troops at the city's gates."

Voln tilted his head backward with a groan. "When can I rest?"

"You've rested your entire life. It's time for you to become the leader you claim to be."

Voln nodded. "I expect a feast after this round. What do you want me to tell the Thanes?"

"I don't want you to tell the Zhaes Thanes anything. Inform our commanders in each Canton to leave a few troopers to contain the Zhaes Thanes and then send the remaining soldiers to the center of the city. Inform them we will join the central mobs to take the city at sundown."

Voln reached his final Canton–the Canton of Diplomacy–with what seemed to be an hour remaining until sundown. As he approached the building, he returned to his human form.

No one was attacking the Canton, but a group of fifteen soldiers in front of the building suggested that there had been a fight.

Two Sleffmen soldiers recognized him from the previous visit and stepped aside for him to enter.

"Where's Port?" Voln shouted.

Allegiant guards stood still along the inside wall.

"Did you hear me, you perding kulfs?"

"In the upper chamber, first to the right... I believe... um...sir.".

Voln continued up the main stairway with his head held high.

Though the exterior varied, each of the Zhaes Canton interiors was modeled after a single design. The Zhaesmen prided themselves on the intricate details and organizational feats. Voln thought it was lazy. The Tchoyas Cantons were more homely and did not feel like an infirmary.

Port stood among Sleffmen near the back of the chamber.

"Port!" he shouted, pressing through the Sleffmen.

"Sir Voln!" said Port. "Back so soon? Does Thane Stolk have another request?"

"He is ready to storm the *perding* center. He wants us to meet there at sundown. Keep some of your soldiers here to watch over the Zhaesmen in the Canton."

Port called one of his officers. "Gather the free soldiers and inform them of Thane Stolk's command. Make sure you have the rest retain a hold on this Canton." He turned back to Voln. "Does he want the commanding officers to march?"

He shrugged. "I'm only the messenger. You decide for yourself. *I* am joining the action. Waiting is a game for stewards and scholars, not warriors."

⸎⸎⸎⸎⸎⸎⸎ ⸎⸎⸎⸎⸎⸎

Phenmir led a wide caravan of Chussman through cobblestoned streets toward the center of Kzhek.

The evening mist obscured the remaining sunlight.

Two frontmen accompanied Phenmir on each side. Their heads turned back and forth, checking for any threats.

Shouts echoed down through the alleys between the high-reaching buildings. He caught the stench of wood burning as strong as the salty musk of the ocean upon entering Court Gruth. The outer sectors of Kzhek were somewhat damaged with waste buildup, but the portions nearest the center were reminiscent of the Sleff alleyways synonymous with negligence. Large pieces of stone had fallen from the walls, cracking the streets beneath. Burned remains of torches and propaganda fliers left ash and charcoal to stain the corners. Shops and stands were long abandoned. Phenmir had never harbored a liking for Kzhek, nor had he for any Zhaes city, but he felt undeniable grief for the tarnished beauty.

The clamor increased as they approached the end of the long street. Orange glimmers shimmered on the left side of the road. Phenmir called the militia to a halt, looking past the corner with his two guards. The sight before him was as he had expected, but exponentially larger than before. It seemed as if a fourth of the city's population filled the square.

"*These* are Zhaesmen?" the soldier to his right said with wide eyes. "I've never seen them like this."

"Most are Zhaesmen," replied Phenmir. He turned back to the troops behind him and bid the guards follow.

"Hold strong as we enter!" shouted Phenmir. He led his share of the Allegiant army into the city's center.

The mob turned to watch their army entering through the southeast passage. The central square was the size of a small village.

He marched to the southwest corner of the square, allowing the troops to file in and stand aside for the next command. The closest rejectionists were within speaking distance, but far enough out to allow a reaction of self-defense if they were to attack.

"What is this?" a Zhaesman asked.

Phenmir pressed forward as the crowd continued to shout.

"Have you come to punish our call for freedom?"

"Here to claim more children to satiate your appetite?"

The entire crowd seemed to stare at them, with shouts growing louder. Phenmir looked to the Chussman at his right. "Blow it."

The Chussman reached into his rucksack and removed a horn that reminded Phenmir of those of the Chuss dune rams. He placed the tip against his lips and blew with the strength of a Zhaes monsoon, capturing the entire square's attention with its call. The horn did not earn complete silence, but many quieted their bellows to lend their ears.

"Zhaesmen!" shouted Phenmir. "Rejectionists! Allies! We of Chuss, Tchoyas, and Sleff plead your cause!"

The voices of the rioters seemed to sound more confused than angry.

Phenmir observed their reactions with skepticism. "Who is leading this rebellion?"

Phenmir waited with firm posture. All he could hear was murmuring and the occasional shout.

Staring into their midst, he saw three figures proceeding forward, two of them dressed in a noble garb that signified them as laborers from a Zhaes Canton.

The wall of Zhaesmen split to let the three forward. The frontmost Zhaesmen held staffs and blades in protective stances.

The Chussman at Phenmir's side took a step diagonally to stand before Phenmir in a guard stance.

"Stand back, Chussman," said Phenmir. He stepped forward. *Remain peaceful and confident.*

The trio stopped a few paces away from Phenmir. In the center stood a Zhaesman in torn and stained clothes, though his confidence was unwavering. The two at his side were Zhaeswomen adorned in Canton garb.

"What do you want?" one of the Zhaeswomen asked.

Phenmir was about to speak, but stopped as the square grew even louder.

They all turned at corners of the square to view an army approaching from the west and east corners. Thane Holmn led an army of Tchoyasmen on one side, while the other group was a mix of Allegiant soldiers. Troops from the city gates had joined their efforts.

"We have come to help your cause prevail." Phenmir said.

The trio's six eyes mingled in silent discussion.

"And why should we trust you?" the Zhaesman asked.

"My name is Phenmir Stolk, Chuss Thane of Harmony, and high advisor to the commander of The Harmony Allegiant."

"The what?" asked the Zhaesman

"The Harmony Allegiant. Are you not all members?"

Two of them whispered to each other, but one of the Zhaeswomen started forward. Half of her head was shaved, while the other side reached her shoulder.

Phenmir took another step forward. "The Harmony Allegiant is a coalition of Courts in favor of overturning the harvesting laws throughout all of Facet. We are here to help you win the battle that you have been fighting for so long."

"And what do you want from us?" a Zhaesmwoman asked.

The one with the shaved hair stepped closer to Phenmir. "Colrig sent you?"

Phenmir breathed easier than he had all day. "Yes! Yes, he did!"

"What are you talking about?" the Zhaesman asked the Zhaeswoman with the shaved hair.

"These are the people that I was talking about."

"The Sleffman?" he asked.

"Yes. This is what we have been hoping for. Laeih is with us." She turned back to Phenmir. "You actually made it here?"

"Colrig said that he is bringing more people," said Phenmir. "We already have most of the Canton's under our control, but we have to act fast. The nobility is planning to attack."

"But you said that you had them under your control?" the Zhaesman said.

"It is not enough to hope that capturing the Cantons stopped their attack. We need to leave the city center and plot elsewhere. It is not safe here."

Feigned valor fled the trio's eyes. Gasps and anxious whispers made their way through the crowd behind them.

"Where did you learn this?" asked the other Zhaeswoman.

"Your Court's Caser fled to our temporary settlement to plead for an armistice. She knew little of our goal, but pleaded for us to remove ourselves from the conflict as the Zhaes nobility threatened to reign terror on your movement. They wished to prevent your progression and any replication of your efforts."

"You really think we should join them?" the Zhaesman asked the Zhaeswoman with the shaved hair.

"We have to," she replied. "This is what we have been fighting for. Years have led to this moment." She turned to the Zhaeswoman and whispered. They both nodded. She faced Phenmir and raised a fist and shouted. "Hail the Harmony Allegiant!"

An uproar grew throughout the mob, growing as more joined in. Rejectionists inspired their neighbors and raised their torches and weapons with a shared shout. The Zhaesman in the back of the crowd joined in. They would learn the reason for rejoicing soon enough.

Phenmir raised his fingers to his forehead and pointed them in a steeple upward. The crowd stared at his hands as he formed the Zhaes salute. Their uproar doubled in enthusiasm as each man and woman in the square joined in the riotous shout.

CHAPTER TWENTY-SIX

THE WORTH OF A PRECEPTOR

C ourt Tchoyas was similar to Kzhek, but Fheo missed his home. Youth had limited his experiences abroad. Compared to Aerhee, he was a pond insect, while she was a serpent of the seas. Kzhek was comfortable and had all that a Zhaesman could need.

The Krall had offered him a single ghete, which he accepted. He would have much rather had a carriage. He had ridden a ghete once as a younger boy, but their stench clouded over his memory of how to control them.

Though he had left in the chill of the morning, citizens had already filled the streets. THe Holdae season had begun, giving a glimpse of the oncoming season of Zeemer to close the year. Despite the chill, they still had time before the first snowfall.

Fayis Ghete, he read from a hanging wooden sign of dark wood. He approached the stable to stand behind a line of three Tchoyasmen. The

Fayis stable appeared to have at least ten ghete, though he could not tell if any shared space.

"Next!" the rancher called, and two Tchoyasmen before him proceeded. The procession continued until he met the stableman, who wore the mask of a burly man that reminded him of a Gorger.

"A Zhaesman." the stableman said, "to Kzhek?"

Fheo nodded.

"One zhon," he held out his hand.

Only one? He held out the note given to him by Krall Trhet.

Sinewy fingers grasped the parchment. The stableman looked at him with a skeptical glare. Though obscured by the dim light, Fheo could see the man's eyes widen.

"On the Krall's errand?" He reached into the key slots. "Number four should suit you. She's young and can make the trip to Kzhek quicker than most of the older steeds."

He nodded as he took the keys from the man's fingers.

The two men who had stood before him in line were still preparing their ghete as he entered the stable. Fheo approached his own steed with slow steps to observe the riders. He knew riding would return to him once he began, but was hesitant to begin.

He was relieved to see that his steed was already bridled with a modest saddle. It was not cushioned, rather, it was composed of cracked leather, though he could not expect otherwise with a public breed.

The rider to his right fed his steed with a dead mink from a feeding barrel and did so three more times before mounting his steed.

A young stableboy with a fish mask opened the gate.

The ghete growled as Fheo approached. *Feed and please*, he remembered, stepping backward to retrieve the ghete's meal. His hand touched each mink for only a second as he tossed them forward to be devoured by the ghete. Fheo stepped forward with a frown, but mounted the ghete with ease.

The fish-masked boy stopped before the ghete. "Do you plan to stay? You might want to unlatch the steed before you try to leave."

Fheo glanced back, embarrassed to realize that the chain had not yet been unlatched. He attempted to dismount the ghete in an awkward manner, but the fish masked boy quickly recognized his unease and unlatched it for him.

The beast ran free and fast. Fheo panicked and pulled on the bridle to a halt. He leaned forward with slight pressure on his heels. The ghete responded with a trot, then moved toward Fheo's tug. The technique returned to him like hearing a favored bard's tale after five years without it. As the city gates opened before him, he conducted the ambition of his steed and flew forward like a diving falcon.

❧❦❧ ❦❧❦

Aerhee did not mind having the room to herself. She enjoyed the company of others but felt it more productive to spend one's spare time studying rather than discussing gossip or material interests. Krall Trhet remained austere with her confinement but provided reading materials upon request. He spoke to her on rare occasions and avoided specifying his intentions.

She had time for reflection, time to search for her purpose in the collapse of Facet. *Why am I here, Laeih?* she prayed. *Why have I been treated as filth in my pursuit of peace?*

She had spent the better part of four hours reading the financial history of Court Sleff and left the tome feeling no less educated about them. She paced the chamber and was drawn to watch the passing clouds through the window.

The sun had fallen beyond the horizon. A flock of birds flew in the distance, Gruth fowls who had begun their migration west before the Zeemer months began. She admired their harmony, each one relying on the other as they flew, and thought of Zeir, her husband. She had directed their flock of two, too often ignoring his wishes. Still, he stayed at her side. *I'm such a prideful kulf.*

Her husband's image haunted her as she saw his patient smile engraved into the low-hanging Tchoyas clouds. *Zeir.* He was always kind and obedient when she was not, like the love child of Chuss and Zhaes saints.

A tear slid down her cheek for her ignorance and selfishness. She treated him like an object to drive her goals forward. She had always planned on their marriage remaining regardless of her choices. Zeir was a patient man, but even the best people break. She needed to repair the cracks that she had made through ignorance. It had been months, maybe years, since she felt this way. She longed for a warm embrace, only crying more when she knew it was beyond her reach.

evening alone for her embrace, though it would never come.

Tears changed from a drip into a stream. *Why am I seeing this now when I should be worried about war?* Perhaps seeing the compassion of others towards unborn children had caused her to question her morality. She was so absorbed by Zhaes law that she had forgotten the reason the law was given. Could Laeih forgive her? Could Zeir?

She remembered Zeir courting her. He had never disappointed her, spoken of her poorly. *She* had disappointed him, spoken of him poorly, and neglected him. She had never lost love for him. It had only since been buried what she had thought was important in life.

She laughed through tearful eyes at the idiosyncrasy of her emotionality.

She remembered tears and pain. It was not the pain of a wound, but that of bereavement; a girl's first loss.

Memories of her parents returned to her

Was she ready to face the occurrences of the past once again? The sins of the Patriarchy? The *bereavement* that has never left her whole?

She accepted the path of her thoughts. In her mind, she saw the bronze statue of a man in agony, the same statue that remains before the Zhaes Canton of Veneration. She surrendered to the pressure of tears.

CHAPTER TWENTY-SEVEN

A VOICE IN THE SHADOWS

Yetrik sat against a chamber wall alongside the underlings of the Canton, each one bound at the wrists. Blinking, he watched the Sleffmen soldiers clutching spears.

Someone had awoken him early. Sleffmen had flooded the Canton and taken him captive. *What have they done to Royss? What of the other Cantons? Had Semi been able to leave the city before its infiltration?*

Rumors of war had not left him at ease, but the reality of the situation confounded him. *How will the Zhaes Thanes control the mobs now?*

❦

Ghael, an armored Sleffwoman, passed through the halls of the Zhaes Canton of Diplomacy, carrying thick manacles.

Thane Leisa, though a captive, had requested to use the privy. Ghael was to be her escort, keeping the Thane, bound by a small chain at the ankles.

"Waste removal," said Ghael as she stepped up to the Thane and knelt to bind her ankles.

"Thank Laeih." said Thane Leisa.

The stairs took twice as long to ascend, but they reached her privy in time. They entered together, turning to assure that they remained alone.

"Well executed, Ghael." Sheath said as she turned to face the guard with a smirk.

"Whole is the Holy, Thane Leisa." The Sleffwoman's face turned pale as she shifted her skin to reveal her true Zhaes complexion. She stared at the wrapping over Thane Sheath Leisa's eye.

Sheath smiled. "I knew having a Shiftling so close to me would become useful, though I noticed your gait that revealed you as a Zhaeswoman. I have never seen such eloquence from a Sleffwoman."

"At least I have some of their armor. I had to take out one of their guards to retrieve it. Have you learned anything by reading the rebels? How should I free you?" Ghael asked.

"Don't worry about me right now. I need you to focus on Thane Royss Belik, in the Canton of Agriculture. He is leading the plans to stop the riots, and I am sure he will be able to find a way around these captors." Sheath arched her back.

"What do you want me to tell him?" Ghael took a piece of parchment from her pocket and began to write.

"A Sleffman named Port is holding this Canton. I had no problem reading him. He had no idea that I was a Feelman."

Ghael nodded

"These invaders call themselves the 'Harmony Allegiant.' Not only do they seek to aid the dissenters of our Court, but they aim to abolish harvesting throughout all of Facet."

Sheath waited for Ghael to write before continuing.

"If you see anyone leaving these Cantons, that is because they are sending most of their troops to the center. They hope to join with the dissenters of our Court to control the Cantons and the Krall's palace. Make sure Royss knows about this, we should be able to stop them before they have complete control. Free Royss if you can."

Ghael finished writing, then looked up to Sheath. "Anything else?"

Sheath shook her head. "Be swift now. Our best chance at success is to hit their army when they are all together."

Ghael returned to the guise of a Sleffwoman as she guided Sheath back to her seat of confinement.

***

Ghael approached the guards that stood before the Canton of Agriculture. One a Tchoyasman and the other a Chussman.

"I have a message from Sir Port," she said. "It concerns the movement to the city center. He requested that I deliver it immediately."

They looked at each other and opened the doors.

She paced ahead, trying to control her anxiety to avoid alerting anyone. She needed to find Royss. While wandering the second floor, she heard his voice and followed it to a study. Royss was bound to a chair near the back wall. Two guards stood at his side.

"What do you want?" asked one of the guards, a Sleffman.

"Port wants me to deliver this note to the Thane." Ghael held up a small sheet of parchment.

"And what might that be?"

"A proposal for the Zhaes Thanes."

"Let me see," the Sleffman took the note from her hand and began to read aloud. "*Cattle trade in the north...embargo against Priess...*" He handed it back to Ghael. "I don't know what any of this means."

"That is because it is for the Thane of *Agriculture*, not you." Ghael dropped her hands to her side and slid the note into her pocket, and grabbed a different one with the same shape and tears. "Can I give it to him, Sleffman?"

The guard nodded.

She offered it to Royss, noting that the guards were not watching, and briefly changed the skin color of her finger.

Royss suppressed a grin, though it bled lightly through his lips. Unable to retrieve the note with his bound hands, she held it up to his face for him to briefly read.

Sleff, Tchoyas, and Chuss have invaded
Most of the Cantons captured
Palace is the last target.
They are flooding the city center to gain Zhaes allies
Act swift

"Can I write a response?" asked Royss.

Ghael removed a new parchment slip from her pocket and handed it to the Thane with a writing utensil. He wrote with difficulty as his wrists remained bound.

He handed her the parchment and dismissed her.

The sun had fallen past midday as she left the Canton. Guards circled the building, causing her to proceed to a distant corner of the property to read in. She removed the note.

There is a hovel south of the courtyard
Enter, find the cellar and the Gorger within
If he is free, have him gather the others to free us and seize the center
Heard them talk. Haleness is still free
Tywing can access the equipment for control of the center
Seek him after the cellar

❦ ❦

Ghael returned the note to her pocket and followed its instructions to find the Gorger. *Why does Royss have some Gorger hidden in a cellar?*

When she arrived at the hovel that Royss had described, she found the courtyard empty of enemy patrolmen. A lock hung from the hovel door's handle but had been left open. Wooden shelves with hoes and shovels lined each wall and stood guard over a square panel on the floor. She reverted to her natural Zhaes self and lifted the panel to reveal a lantern-lit staircase.

She heard heavy footsteps walking towards her.

"What is it, Royss? I already..." The Gorger stopped to stare at her. She brushed aside her black hair. He squinted and scratched his head. "You seem familiar? Have we met? Are you an Endowed?"

"Shiftling," she replied, easing to the bottom step. "We probably met during training."

"No... I remember you! You courted Foreil!"

"That dull Gorger?" blush reddened her cheeks, "I mean, I–"

"Yeah, not the brightest. We spar sometimes. Why are you here?"

"Zhaes has been invaded, and Royss needs your help."

"Invaded? I thought we were the ones who planned an attack?" She noticed the bags beneath his eyes. She nodded. "Well, I..." he stared at the boiling pot on the fire behind him. "I can be ready soon. Where is Royss?"

"Captive," she replied and handed him the note.

"Very well," he said with a sigh that raised his shoulders.

"Why are you in this cellar? Royss can't treat his Endowed that poorly."

"He didn't want people to know that he was gathering the city's Gorgers." He returned the note.

"So the 'others' that he wrote about are the city's Gorgers?"

The Gorger nodded.

"Well, once you take care of that, Royss needs your help to free him. I heard he's the key to saving our city."

"Or so he thinks, though I doubt the kulf is capable," the Gorger laughed. "I'll see it taken care of. So it looks like he wants you to deal with the Thane Tywing in Canton of Haleness? My Laeih guide you. What was your name again?"

"Ghael, and yours?"

"Taeih." He smiled and gave her the Zhaes salute. She returned the sign and ran back up the stairwell.

⁓⁓⁓⁓

Ghael's side ached as she ran to a gradual stop outside of the Canton of Haleness. Royss was right, the Canton was free of invaders. No enemy soldiers stood outside of the Canton and it seemed untouched compared to the other Cantons.

She entered, reverted to her true identity and removed her helm to avoid questions. "Take me to Thane Tywing!" She shouted to the first Zhaesman she saw.

"What do you need with the Thane?" an elderly man asked.

She approached him and tried to tone down her voice. "The Cantons have been—"

"Seized by invaders. So we have heard. Thane Tywing is safe."

"I have a message from Thane Belik." She removed the note. "Follow me."

They proceeded down the hall to the Thane's study. The old man's wrinkled hands pulled the door's handle and gestured for her to enter. Three guards stood on each side of the Thane, who sat behind a desk.

"Ghael?" Thane Tywing stood.

She was surprised that he remembered her name, only having worked together a handful of times. She handed the crumpled note to the Thane.

"Royss needs you to lead the offense."

His eyes dashed back and forth as he read. "*Perd me.*" He turned to the guards on his left. "You three, prepare the ghete. Ten will suffice." His focus returned to Ghael. "You are coming with me."

❦

The Gorger Taeih ran to the outskirts of Kzhek, away from the rebel forces, and entered a small district on the northern border.

The district was forgotten by most of Kzhek who saw the place as a hive for vagabonds and criminals. The Zhaes nobility neglected anything with an undesirable reputation, hence its perpetual existence as a wasted property. It was the ideal location to hide a private Gorger force near the city's hub. Royss and Taeih had sent for the city's Gorgers to gather there two days before.

Once he arrived, he called everyone to gather.

"Endowed brethren and sisters," Taeih shouted. "The time is upon us to defend our Court from the heretics who seek to disrupt our order!"

The Gorgers shouted, but Taeih raised his hands to quiet them.

"Royss has called us to defend the city. They are sending the rest of the city's guards to join us to defend and fight. Tchoyas, Chuss, and Sleff terrorists have already entered our city and have taken our leaders hostage. A select few of you will join me in freeing Royss alongside any other Thanes that he deems useful before the city is freed. Do not *seek* to murder but take lives when necessary to preserve our Court!" He saluted them. "Whole is the Holy!"

"Whole is the Holy!" returned the crowd.

※※⇝⇝ ⇜⇜⇜⇜

Rumbling walls and the clamor of dozens of footsteps caught everyone's attention. Yetrik sat up and adjusted his posture, having grown increasingly tired and anxious. The captives shared unsettled glances while Yetrik directed his attention to the Rebel soldiers. They talked with one another, concern obvious on their faces.

"Remain still!" shouted one of the Sleffmen.

Loud footsteps and shouts sounded behind the closed doors.

Another Sleffman soldier ran to hold the door, but was thrown back as the door broke from its hinges and giant Zhaesmen stormed into the room.

Zhaes Gorgers.

"Stand down!" shouted a Sleffman. "We're armed!" He removed a hand spear from the sheath across his back.

"You take the right side," said the first Gorger, as he seized the soldiers to his left. He blocked the Sleffman's spear with braced gauntlets and grabbed the spear, breaking it like a twig. The Zhaesman's giant hands picked up the soldier and used him as a projectile against the other soldiers, who had not yet armed themselves.

Yetrik watched with a combination of fear and relief as the Zhaes Gorgers disarmed and incapacitated their captors until a pile of unconscious Sleffmen lay in the corner of the room.

"Thank you Zhaesmen. Praise be to Laeih for your divine gifts!" said a spectacled, middle-aged woman.

"Did Royss send you? Is he safe?" Yetrik asked, as a Gorger untied his bindings.

"Yes, and yes. Our Gorgers are freeing those in other Cantons." The Gorger proceeded down the line, looking at Yetrik as each binding fell loose. "Royss is likely free from capture by now."

Conflict continued to reverberate throughout the walls of the Canton. Rebel soldiers tried to fight Gorgers in groups, but even five Sleffmen were no challenge to an Endowed.

Yetrik felt safe with the Gorgers at his side. The stories proved true. Not only were they as strong as the arm of the gods, but they were strategic and calculated, never falling victim to fear. It was a common misconception that Gorgers were dull-minded compared to the other Endowed. Brutes have often been associated with physical strength, compensating for a diminished mental capacity. That was far from true. Their enhanced digestion from their additional intestine not only absorbed nutrients for the exponential growth of their muscles, but also increased their mental capabilities. As a fortified soldier and a cunning strategist, Gorgers were made to win wars.

Yetrik descended to the first floor to find Royss, free of his bindings, speaking with Taeih.

"The Gruthman survived the raid!" chuckled Taeih as Yetrik approached.

"Good to see you again," said Yetrik. "What now?"

Royss stepped up to Yetrik, "We sent the other Gorgers elsewhere, but they will not seize the center until the combustibles are set."

"You have the combustibles on hand?" asked Yetrik.

"Not with me. A Shiftling messenger has left to employ Thane Tywing to see that the center is armed to decimate the rebels."

Decimate? "What are we to do?" asked Yetrik? "Arm ourselves and join the guards and Gorgers? I warn you, Royss, I was trained in the way of the quill and never in the way of the sword."

Royss chortled. "I have better plans for you, Gruthman."

❦

Ghael rode with Thane Tywing to the city's edge, beneath the high walls.

"What is this?" she shouted through the rush of the wind as she embraced his back on their shared ghete.

"One of the city's largest barracks. Seems our oversized force is paying off. I admit that I was a critic of our taxes being spent to fund them. I never thought they would be used for more than fear-mongering petty thieves." He shrugged. "I assume that the invaders have attacked the others, but we have disguised the appearance of this hall to distract unwanted visitors." They approached the east wall as the ghete slowed near the entrance.

Thane Tywing straightened and unclipped his boots from the saddle. "We had some petty workers place the combustibles throughout the city center. They were disguised as dissenters and had no problem fitting in. Our guards in these barracks know how to trigger the command and will finish the job. Though destruction is bound to occur, they were placed in a manner to deal minimal destruction to the central architecture while ensuring an effective offense against the mobs."

"When are they going to set them off?" Ghael asked.

"Soon." The Thane dismounted the steed and pulled it by its reins to a small archway on the side of the entrance. It was no stable, but served to hold the ghete. He tied it to a pole, and it sat with unquestioned obedience as they entered the barracks.

She found hoards of guards within, busy donning their armor and preparing their weapons. Their armor shone brighter than the usual guards throughout Kzhek. The invaders' armor seemed like children's clothing in comparison. Even in acts of war and inevitable violence, the

Zhaesmen sought to glorify their deity through proper wear that shamed the dissenters.

"Zhaesmen!" called Thane Tywing, attracting the attention of the soldiers. "Zhaesmen!" He called three more times to collect the crowd's attention. "Now is your time to protect Kzhek, to retake our beloved capital. The other legions will soon storm the city center. Utility troop, trigger the combustibles. Everyone else, finish off the remaining dissenters. Whole is the Holy!"

"Whole is the Holy!" they responded, each one returning the Zhaes salute, as shown by Thane Tywing. He walked away from the troops to approach the exit.

"Should we stay with them to see your commands executed, Thane?" asked Ghael.

"The battlefield is the home of the soldiers, not their leaders. The Thanes are needed elsewhere."

Ghael turned back to face the preparing troops, knowing that many of them would leave their spouses as widows and widowers before the next sunrise. She wanted to intervene, stop the chaos, or do anything to prevent suffering. She had seen too much pain in her city. There was nothing for her to do but hope that her leaders had the people's best interest in mind. *Laeih preserve us.*

CHAPTER TWENTY-EIGHT

SANGUINEOUS SORROW

Phenmir sat among the Thanes of the Allegiant and the leaders of the Zhaes rejectionists. They sat on large stones that had fallen from the central architecture. "Aside from rioting, what have you done to progress your cause in your Court?"

"Have you seen the ruins of the Canton of Endowment?" asked a Zhaeswoman with suppressed repugnance. "We know, as you do, that the Court will only fall once we have brought the nobility to its knees."

Phenmir shook his head. "I can see your work, but destruction is not our goal. We want a new order in Zhaes, not a graveyard."

"They're harder to command than you would hope, Chussman." said the Zhaeswoman who had half of her head shaved. "We try to control them, but they are blinded by rage. It's gone beyond the Allegiant's goals."

"Which is why we must act fast to get rid of the mob mentality," said Phenmir. "Once we have the city under our control, we will no longer need riots. We all need to remember that Kzhek is not our only goal. How have you dealt with the Zhaesmen who do not want to join your riots?"

"People fled the center as the riots grew. Few people live in the center. Most of the buildings are business or governmental facilities. Their workplaces became unsafe, so they fled to do their work elsewhere. If we can keep any battles in the city center, we can avoid hurting the city's inhabitants."

"Except for those who oppose you?"

The Thanes stood as the floor rumbled.

"What is it?" said Phenmir. He pressed through the troops, trying to find the source of the commotion. He grabbed the shoulder of a shouting Zhaes rejectionist. "What do you see?"

"They are back, sir. They have attempted previously, but they have blocked the streets this time!" The Zhaesmen spoke with dire anxiety and moved as a child, escaping his mother's embrace.

"Who? Tell me clearly, Zhaesman!"

"The city guards! Their legions have grown!"

"Calm yourself. We have been preparing for this."

The rejectionist nodded but was no calmer. The Thanes of Tchoyas had sent bureaucrats to obtain statistics related to the total Zhaes troops. If their report was accurate, the Allegiant outnumbered the city's guards at a four-to-one ratio if the Zhaesmen had sent every trooper in Kzhek. Phenmir guessed that they would send fewer than half their men, only to intimidate the invaders.

Phenmir ran to find the other Thanes, commanding them to prepare their troops for defensive maneuvers. Six Allegiant legions gathered in block formations to surround and protect the Zhaes rejectionists. Each of the Allegiant Courts was represented with two legions led by a chief officer or Thane of their Court.

The Allegiant soldiers tried to gather into their respective legions, but the Zhaes rejectionsists lost every sense of order. People ran into each other, knocking one another down.

"Desert flower!" Phenmir shouted.

"Desert flower!" His command echoed over the crowd as the officers repeated it. Allegiant troops shouted to push the Zhaesmen towards the center.

Each Allegiant legion surrounded the most vulnerable Zhaesmen, while some joined the Allegiant troops. The legions formed into blocks and surrounded the circle in groups like petals on a flower. In their formation, they were able to move outward if necessary, with the entire field in the Allegiant's view.

As the troops fell into line, Phenmir gazed at the alleyways and streets that fed into the central sector. The polished sheen of the guards' armor shimmered under the misty moonlight to decorate their condescension to a predisposed victory. Though they were visible throughout the central square, they halted near the final steps into the square itself. Their taunt called the Allegiant troops forward in anger and frustration.

"Halt!" shouted Phenmir as the troops charged towards the Zhaes guard forces. "Hold your charges!"

Other captains called for a halt as well, to no avail.

All logic flees before the temptress of vengeance.

Phenmir stood still as bodies slammed his shoulders forward to chase Zhaesmen, forcing him forward in their chaotic rush

As the Allegiant troops approached streets leading from the center, Zhaes guards withdrew. The Allegiant troops continued their relentless pursuit, following the Zhaesmen into the streets.

A loud rumble echoed in the distance, like the bang of a ritual drum.

Phenmir shook, looking in each direction for the source of the rumble.

The sound continued, though it approached their proximity with each rumble. His eyes fell to the cobbled street as the sound shook the ground.

The quakes turned to the sound of crumbling rock as if a mountain were splitting.

The tumult of collapsing buildings assaulted his ears.

We captured the Cantons. That should have stopped the–

He covered his head as the clamor approached the alley before him. Stones fell from above. Rubble pelted him like hail.

A deafening blast shook his senses.

He fell with a plume of smoke, like a gust of wind to a frail dandelion. Heat resonated from the source of the sound. He held himself tight as the quake felled the surrounding troops. His ears rang with the screech of a banshee.

❧❧❧❧ ❦❦❦❦

Port fell back onto the cobbled street as explosions rattled the street. He rose to stand alongside half of his legion, though the vanguard remained on their knees as the smoke cleared.

The explosions were triggered in a cascade, with five down each alleyway. Each blast injured or killed more Allegiant troopers. The blasts reverberated throughout the square, but the clamor reached a silent conclusion within a minute of their initiation. Cries and moans were muffled by dust plumes and falling stone.

Port blinked to focus his double vision. "Fall back!" he shouted.

He ran towards the center of the square, passing fallen troopers with broken limbs and dust stuck to blood covered faces. He felt a small shimmer of hope as he saw that most of the people were safe in the square's center.

The legions lost their formation and fell into chaos as those who remained standing ran to help the fallen. Port searched for a familiar face, but there were too many among the dead.

He coughed and rubbed his eyes. Zhaesmen marched towards the center, some stepping over the corpses of fallen soldiers and their remaining carnage. Many had survived the violence, or so he hoped, but so many had been desecrated as collateral to the deceptive Zhaes tactics.

The buildings that lined the central square were decimated to crumbling ruins.

"Prepare for offensive maneuvers!" shouted a familiar voice. "Get back into formation and prepare to meet the Zhaes guards!"

Port searched out the call. It was Phenmir. They would not be granted a period of recovery from the assault, nor would they be given a moment to mourn the dead.

"Defend the Allegiant!" Port's voice trembled as he shouted. He coughed on the dust in his throat.

The legions reformed into the flower petal formations the best they could, facing the approaching Zhaesmen from all around.

The Zhaesmen who had fled from the explosions now rushed into the center, blades ready to strike the Allegiant.

Despite the glory of their armor, the Zhaesmen did not seem to fight with the determination that the Allegiant forces had. Many of the Zhaes guards stepped back as they met the Allegiant, letting their allies take the first strike.

Seeds of trauma scattered as the two sides met in inhumane combat. Port pressed forward but fell still as he saw the carnage before him. He stood ten rows behind the front lines, but nobody before him censored the images of nightmares.

Phirman, a Chuss captain two offices below Phenmir, pressed the front lines of their legion forward. His faith taught to avoid harming others in any manner, but his conscience had quickly subsided to numb him from the violence of war.

Ghanmir, his friend since birth, swung a sword as he stood at Phirman's side. They had joined the Allegiant together, supporting each other throughout each hardship of the journey.

Phirman smiled at his friend two paces before him, who felled a Zhaesman with more armor than either of them

Ghanmir advanced to his next opponent and held his right arm up to block the Zhaesman's downward strike.

Phirman impaled a guard and turned to watch his friend claim yet another victory.

Ghanmir failed to predict his opponent's strike and was struck on the crown. The Zhaes blade caught itself in the Ghanmir's skull, losing momentum and stopping between the eyes.

Phirman lost the savor of victory and stumbled back. His sword dropped from shaking palms as he placed his hands on each side of his face. Disoriented as if he had fallen into a dream, he stared at the surrounding carnage to attempt a return to reality. *A moment. A moment was all that was needed to tear him from this world. A moment of war murdered a brotherhood that had spanned decades.*

This was no dream. He was damned to a reality of death and suffering.

"Head up, Chussman!" shouted a soldier, who struck Phirman with a gauntleted fist. "Fight or die!"

Fight and die. He picked up his sword from the ground.

"Forward with Cheric beside you!" called a voice to his left.

Though many more had fallen among the Chuss legion, the Zhaes legion had fallen to half its size.

Phirman noticed Zhaes corpses at his feet. *We're moving forward.*

He tossed his leather cap away and picked up and donned a Zhaes helm. He would not die as easily as Ghanmir had. The man next to him followed Phirman, taking a helm for better protection. Others followed the exchange and pressed on.

Phirman stepped up to face his next opponent, brushing the fallen Chussman to his right.

The Zhaesman before him lifted his face plate to clear his eyes. Tears fell to meet the mucus that dripped from his nostrils. He returned the faceplate to the covering position. "Come fight... you p-p-perding k-kulf." The guard couldn't be much older than twenty. *He's torn. He did not want this. I do not want this.*

Phirman shook with the heat of remorse as he stepped up to strike the Zhaesman. He parried his strike, allowing their eyes to catch each other across from the clashing blades. *Save the Endowers*, he thought with each swing. *Zhaesmen slay the young.* If Phirman was born in the north, he would have been raised alongside this man and forced to accept the procedure of harvesting.

He countered the Zhaesman's cut and swung up with a callous blow to the pit of his arm, cleaving it off like an axe's blow to a weakened branch. His enemy fell to his knees and braced the open wound with a haunting wail. Not allowing himself to share the Zhaesman's grief, Phirman swung at the gap between his opponent's armor into his bare neck. His fists stung as a shock soared upward through the blade. Phirman's blade stopped halfway through the neck as it collided with a piece of armor.

He stared at the body before him, mesmerized by the life that had vanished in a mere instant. Like a roach stepped upon by an ignorant boot.

The next Zhaesman ahead took no note of his fallen comrade.

Phirman looked up at his approaching challenger with time enough to see the shimmer of metal swing in his periphery. Phirman lost his head just as he had taken his opponent's a moment before. The Zhaesman's blade passed through like a scythe to a weary and aged stem.

"The Tchoyas troops have won their engagement, Thane Stolk," said a Chussman of small stature.

Phenmir turned around to identify a boy who appeared to be fourteen or fifteen. He did not wear sufficient armor for a soldier, but enough to prevent most injuries from any rogue arrows.

"Say that again?"

"The northeastern passage, sir. The Tchoyasmen have cleared it. All remaining Zhaes troops fled to save the few lives that remained."

"Steadfast is the Honor!" the Tchoyasman shouted their Ideal. Phenmir felt that he could breathe again, seeing the empty street before the Tchoyasman where Zhaes troops had stood moments before.

"Thane Holmn!" Phenmir shouted as he spotted the Tchoyaswoman with the fanged mask. He shouted again before she heard him and ran to meet.

"Yes, Thane Stolk?"

"Well done, but we still need your help."

"Where do you want us?"

"Have the left flank join the Chuss legion and the right join the Sleff legion."

She nodded and ran back to command her legion.

The Sleff legion was the smallest, but was fortunate to have faced the smallest group of Zhaesmen. The Sleff and Chuss groups pressed onward, but still needed the Tchoyas aid.

As the Tchoyas legion joined the others, they pressed through the Zhaesmen twice as fast. More Zhaesman retreated, and the Allegiant continued to fight. As the final groups of Zhaesmen fled, some of the Allegiant soldiers chased them down, denying them their escape.

The Allegiant troops held their weapons high, rejoicing in their victory.

"Glory to the Harmony Allegiant!" some shouted, while others roared their Court Ideals.

"Steadfast is the Honor!"

"Care is the Creed!"

"Pious is the Giver!"

Even the Zhaes rioters joined in. "Whole is the Holy!"

"Allegiant!" Phenmir shouted. "This is not the end! Hold your rejoicing, we have–"

"Allow us to celebrate, Chussman!" shouted the Sleffmen nearest to him. The surrounding soldiers nodded. "We held off the entirety of the Zhaes force!" Shouts of praise accompanied his Sleff salute with the heels of his palms on his temples and fingers upward like a crown of triumph. "Their explosions were nothing before our might!"

You might not think so once you realize how many of your allies have died. "Are you so foolish to think that was the *entire* Zhaes force? Yield not to an early victory. We have faced only a fraction of the Zhaes soldiers, and I fear the coming wave will be larger than we can bear. Their tacticians have certainly spent the latter weeks studying the works of the strategists of old. Each one speaks that deception is the keystone to victory. The Zhaesmen likely wish to deceive us with an early victory. Remain stalwart, people of the Allegiant!"

Port approached him. Tears in his armor exposed flesh to the cold humidity of the Zhaes evening. "We understand, Thane Stolk, but many have fallen in only our first engagement. Can we not celebrate this small victory?"

"Maintain high spirits," Phenmir replied, "but do not allow pride to create a careless force." Port nodded. "We need to keep our energy up for what is coming. Will you ask the Zhaes rejectionists how they have fed their large party?"

"With pleasure, Thane Stolk."

The sun crept over the horizon and shone through the morning mist like light through an aged chapel window. Many soldiers had fallen asleep, despite the danger of letting their guard down. The few self-proclaimed resilient who remained awake teetered on exhausted feet. They remained in the center to keep their army together. If they spread throughout the city, they would become too vulnerable to Zhaes tactics.

Phenmir slept only for a few hours, switching off with some of the other Thanes, making sure a leader was always ready. He wanted to sleep more, but sleep was a luxury. War was no time for luxury. He spent the energy he had tending to the injuries of the soldiers. He helped those who had a chance at healing. Despite his efforts, some soldiers were injured beyond repair. He focused his efforts on those who had a chance at healing.

The Allegiant troopers who did not want to sleep spent their time combing the square for better equipment from the fallen Zhaesmen. Phenmir only hoped that no Allegiant soldier would be killed by an ally, being mistaken as an enemy. To prevent such a complication, those who took Zhaes armor tied strips of cloth across their helms, shoulders, or weapons. The fabric flew bloody in Chuss-red, flying with a sign of their fallen allies, if not from their own wounds. They hoped that this would prevent allies from killing each other, but they were prone to error in the rage of combat. For this reason, many avoided changing their armor.

He rose to don his helm and cover his silver dreadlocks.

Port stood to meet him. "Thane Stolk, I hope you were able to rest. I have been sure to—"

"Have you rested, Port?" he replied.

"Half an hour or so, sir. Would you like me to prepare the troops?".

Phenmir watched the square, noticing that soldiers spoke quietly amongst themselves while their neighbors slept in slouched positions against fallen rubble. "No," he replied. "Allow them–" He stopped and looked upwards.

"What is it, Thane Stolk? Do–"

"Listen." he whispered with a hand on Port's shoulder and an ear still reaching out in focus. "The northeastern district. Do you hear that?"

Port turned to listen. As their armor clattered with movement, others began to wake.

The sound of raindrops grew into a clatter of steady hail, though the echo was metallic, and the sky was dry.

"Fall into position and arm yourselves!" Phenmir called.

"Have they returned?"

"I'm afraid so," Phenmir's eyes remained fixated on the northeastern passage. "Gather and organize your Sleffmen. I will see that the Tchoyas Thanes are ordering their troops."

"Already at it, Thane Stolk," said a voice behind him. He turned over his shoulder to recognize the angered mask of Thane Holmn. "My admirals have already left for their assigned legions."

Phenmir nodded and dismissed her, leaving himself to command the Chussmen. The Chuss Thanes awaited his direction with their appointed admirals on their sides.

"Thane Stolk!"

Thane Trhet, the Tchoyas Thane of Progress, approached him with ornate armor appropriate for the battlefield as well as a dining hall. He recognized her identity with the memory of the silver lips on her mask.

"Thane Trhet, I have not seen you–"

"I kept myself hidden. Certain Endowed are reserved for matters of intrigue and support rather than combat," she replied.

"You? An Endowed?"

"Yes, but don't worry, I'm loyal to the Allegiant."

"But you're a Tchoyaswoman! An Endowed from a non-harvesting Court!"

"Before our Court decreed complete opposition to harvesting, the Zhaes nobility offered my grandfather, Krall Trhet, a graft. Most of us already opposed harvesting, but my grandfather tries to remain neutral when possible. He gave me the organ. I mourn the child who died for me, but I intend to use the organ for good."

Phenmir nodded.

"Only the other Tchoyas Thanes know what I am. I wouldn't have told you if it was unnecessary. I'm a Foreteller, but my foresights are imperfect. My ability has given me a warning. We *must* hold back the entirety of our strength during this next wave of Zhaes forces."

"Are there more than we feared?"

"I'm not sure, but I know that we cannot exert all of our force. We need to be at the southern city gates soon."

"You suggest we remain idle while troops seize us? I *hear* their approach!"

"You don't need to surrender," she said. "Just be conservative. Hold back."

Phenmir nodded, willing to trust her. "Thank you, Thane Trhet. I will relay your recommendation with the other Thanes in command."

She departed through the crowd of soldiers.

The clamor no longer sounded like rainfall. It was a clear march of armored feet.

"Sleffmen!" Phenmir called. Port and the other two appointed heads of their Court's legion approached the call of their captain. "Stay here while I invite the Tchoyasmen to join us in a brief council."

"But sir, they are nearly here!" Port said.

"We'll have a moment while the troops fall into their formations," Phenmir continued to step away. "Stay here."

Among the Tchoyasmen, he spotted some with silver accents on their masks. *The Thanes.*

"Tchoyas Thanes!"

"Thane Stolk?" asked Thane Holmn.

"Has Thane Trhet given you her warning?"

She shook her head. "No. What do you mean?"

"We can talk about that later. Follow me." He left, and they complied without question.

Phenmir waved for the Thanes and commanders to gather into a circle.

"We have a warning from a Forteller." He ignored the questioning faces of some in the circle. We need to avoid using all of our strength in lieu of preparation for following waves of Zhaesmen.""Why?" asked the Sleffwoman who stood to Port's right.

"Forgive her, Thane Stolk," said Port with a disappointed glare at her.

"We will see soon enough. All I ask is that you trust me."

The circle remained silent and focused.

"Thank you." said Phenmir. "Instruct your legions to kill their enemies when necessary, but to avoid brash combat maneuvers. Command your troops into tight formations. Shield walls, deceptive angles, whatever it takes to wear them down."

Phenmir saluted and dismissed them.

Rows of figures shimmered through the morning haze. Their armor was unblemished, giving credibility to Phenmir's claim that the previous attack included only a small selection of the Zhaes guards.

As the Zhaesmen reached the square, they ran to clash with the Harmony Allegiant.

Phenmir shouted for his troops to prepare themselves while the rightmost army clashed with the invading Zhaesmen.

"*Go—s!*"

He turned his head to identify the call that arose from those fighting for their lives.

"*Gor–s!*"

The Allegiant forces fell back.

"*Gorgers! Zhaes Gorgers!*"

Their shouts were clear as he ran to attend to his allies. Zhaes Gorgers fought alongside the guard forces.

Someone called his name. He turned back to see Thane Trhet parting the crowd as she rode atop a ghete.

"Thane Trhet!" he called. Her ghete accelerated and kicked pebbles up around its pounding paws.

"Mount behind me."

He grabbed her hand and swung himself up behind her. She kicked her heels as soon as he grasped onto the sides of the saddle and fled the combat.

"Don't worry," she said. "We are not defecting our troops in a vulnerable state."

"Then what are we doing?"

"I understand my foretelling now." She said, "I saw you alone at the southern gate. This vision was urgent. I feared that the second wave of Zhaesmen could be our call to the grave.""Why the southern gates?"

"Hold on," she hit her heels to increase the ghete's speed.

The Zhaes public slept–or hid–to avoid the central conflict, leaving the streets desolate.

They reached the southern district of the city within minutes. City walls stood as guardians to any who sought entry, but the gate had already fallen victim to recent destruction.

Beyond the dilapidated gateway, Phenmir faced a battalion of gigantic soldiers, led by a smaller man atop a ghete of an eastern breed, more purple than green.

"Heloath, Phenmir! Perd, you look pitiful. Sorry for the late arrival. Lead us to the center!" The man doffed his helm to reveal his Sleff identity. Colrig had arrived with an army of Sleff Gorgers.

CHAPTER TWENTY-NINE

SPECTACLE OF THE BRONZE TRANSGRESSOR

26 YEARS AGO, COURT ZHAES, KZHEK YEAR 306 IN THE CLERICAL ERA (CL. ER. 306)

Aerhee walked alongside Faeth to the eastern sector of Kzhek, where the Patriarchy of Scholars would hold Derliks's trial. Faeth prayed that representatives from *each* Court would decide his verdict but knew the Zhaesmen felt their views were superior. What should comprise a fair trial at the justice of the Patriarchy would be a biased defacement of a former Priessman. It sickened her to think of her new nation with such disdain, but she could not ignore their prejudice.

They arrived later than the other attendees. While the others were offered ghete carriages, no one felt obliged to treat the family of the guilty party with dignity.

She held Aerhee's hand. Since the ordeal with the Patriarchy, Faeth had become withdrawn from her personal matters. Their cottage was left untidy and the crops in their garden had wilted from neglect.

They held the trial in the Patriarchal chapterhouse in Kzhek, a few buildings west of the Canton of Scholarship.

Attendees left their carriages on the street while they sent their underlings to attend to the needs of the ghete. Aerhee and Faeth ascended the short staircase to enter the building. Faeth opened the door for her daughter, taking a deep breath to calm herself.

The chamber was filled with only five non-Zhaes Scholars, while twenty Zhaes representatives from their brotherhood sat in on high seats. *Is this necessary for such a petty crime?* Not only was the Canton of Scholarship represented, but ten representatives from the Canton of Veneration attended to observe the trial. While the Canton of Veneration oversaw the Court's law, the dictates of the Patriarchy trumped even their word. Derlik sat at the head of the room with his back to the door.

"Seat the Priesswomen in the back left row," spoke the man from the high pulpit. He wore ostentatious robes with bronze embroidery. The Zhaes Thane of Veneration. The robed Gruthman, who sat lower beside him, was dressed in a less ornate manner. Nevertheless, his grab was reminiscent of the standing Zhaesman. Faeth felt a new wave of dread overcome her as her husband faced the judgment of *two* Thanes of Scholarship. The Gruthman was more likely to be magnanimous, but Court Gruth still harbored a disdain for Priessmen.

Aerhee held onto Faeth's hand as they took their seats.

The two guards who stood at the entrance shut the doors.

"Whole is the Holy!" shouted the standing Scholar.

"Whole is the Holy!" repeated the crowd with the Zhaes salute. Aerhee complied with the ritualistic sign of loyalty; Faeth remained still, with sullen eyes fixated on the orator.

"Heloath and welcome. I pray that the justice of Laeih will be present during this trial. As Thane of Scholarship, I will join the high-most members of the Patriarchy on the final verdict for the guilty party." His eyes turned to grasp Faeth's gaze. "Two arguments will be offered. After they are presented, the Scholars will exit to discuss the verdict, which we will decide ourselves. There is no need to waste excess time on narratives and pleas, only facts and evidence. The trial will be concluded before the end of the hour." He opened his eyes wide to prompt a response from Faeth and was pleased when she offered a reluctant nod to confirm her understanding.

He smiled and continued. "Thane Haeth Eiph, of the Canton of Veneration, will present the condemning evidence. The guilty party will then have a moment to defend himself. Thane Eiph, the pulpit is yours." He stepped down to face the audience and continued to stand with forced rigidity.

"Derlik Kleeh, the Priessman seated before you, is said to be charged with the following crimes: perjury, unauthorized immigration, fraud, usage of counterfeit currency, evasion of the law, heresy, transgression of the laws of Laeih, and treason."

Faeth opened her eyes and mouth, aghast at the claims against her husband. He was imperfect, but they took a single act to be perceived as disgracing the entire Zhaes law. *All we ever wanted was to be a part of you.*

"Derlik Kleeh entered our Court without legal allowance and sought to deceive our people into believing that he and his family were Zhaes-born. It should be recognized that his counterfeit money was produced by a sect of Scholar dissenters known as *the Bronze Seers*." Some in the audience gasped. "These dissenters seek to corrupt the Patriarchy to utilize its authority for their gain."

Faeth lowered her eyes, dispelling any remaining hope for mercy. She could not expect justice to be dealt with on a broken scale. She had never heard of these *Bronze Seers*. Surely Derlik had no desire to see the downfall of the Patriarchy.

"The Priessman and his spouse," the Thane continued, "entered our Court with their daughter to promote Priess influence in Kzhek and likely advocate the cause of the Bronze Seers. Many have noticed that many Zhaesmen have defected to Court Priess in recent years. We cannot allow the people of Facet to believe that we are vulnerable to such cultural persuasions. I propose that this Priessman be punished sufficiently that we might not see his actions repeated. Should we set him free, we allow an associate of false Scholarhood and an advocate of Priess propaganda to continue his debauchery."

The prosecutor returned to her seat. Two Scholars turned Derlik's seat to face the audience.

"Fellow Zhaesmen," began Derlik, "yes I call you my fellow men and women because I have become Zhaes by principle and faith. If anyone is being deceived, it is you. I paid for my family to immigrate with counterfeit funds because we had no other way of entry. I knew nothing of these *Bronze Seers*, the coins were merely given to me by another Priessman. We were taxed and charged more than the worth of our belongings and had no hope of escaping Court Priess. You claim we are loyal to Court Priess, but their hedonism is the very reason we left. I wanted to raise my daughter in your faith, to provide her with stability and structure. I confess my usage of counterfeit funds, but all other claims against me have no ground. Yes, I may be guilty of this, but I don't deserve the punishment of a murderer or traitor. Let Laeih's will guide your verdict. Zhaesmen, I–"

"Enough," shouted the Thane of Scholarship. "Thane Eiph, do you have any concluding statements?"

She stood and turned to face the audience. "This Priessman has been charged with deception and continues to lie for any chance of avoiding punishment. Do not be deluded by the deceitful heretic who sits before you."

Faeth felt like crying out in condemnation, but sat paralyzed.

"Thank you, Thane Eiph. The council will now convene. We ask that the occupants of this room remain seated while we conclude the verdict." The Scholars left with heads held high.

The door closed behind the last member of the party; gossip arose throughout the chamber with echoes of whispered hatred. Faeth lifted her head up but was only left with dire gloom as she saw her husband sobbing.

※※⟫⟫⟩ ⟨⟨⟨⟨⟨⟨

The room went silent as the Scholars returned. Thane Eiph stood beside the Thane of Scholarship, who stepped up to the podium.

"The charge is as follows," he read from their declaration. "Derlik Kleeh of Court Priess is to be given a public execution for transgression of Zhaes law. This will be held before the Canton of Veneration as a display of Zhaes law to any who would dare to repeat his sin of Priess propaganda. The event is to be held tomorrow at midday. His spouse and child will not be held accountable, but this tale will serve to warn their fellow Priessmen of the consequences of such a transgression. Should the woman and child oppose us further, they will be met swiftly by a sword of justice." He rolled the parchment into a scroll and stepped down from the podium.

The Scholars dismissed the audience and took Derlik through the left chamber. The procession of Zhaesmen departed, returning to their previous gossip like a divorced drunk to his mead. Though they dressed as nobles, their tongues spoke with more spite and improper judgment than schoolchildren.

Aerhee and Faeth remained seated in the empty chamber. Aerhee embraced her mother, who sat with silent tears streaming down her worn cheeks. Faeth embraced her with a single arm. She wanted to mourn with her daughter. She wished to scream and let the tears roar out like the waves of the Gruth sea, but she remained silent, frozen in anger.

⁂

The gloom of the following morning forbade the sun, as was the pattern with most days in Kzhek.

A vast crowd had formed around the Canton of Veneration. More joined in like the buildup of sticks in a dam as they noticed Zhaes nobles and an abundance of Patriarchal Scholars.

Aerhee held her mother's hand. Her hand felt lifeless. Aerhee did not know how else to explain it. Her mother seemed distant ever since the Patriarchy had taken her father. Faeth forced their way to the front of the crowd.

Aerhee looked ahead to see her father standing immobile, with raised arms. Above him stood a wooden arch with a smoking cauldron hanging from its top.

What is happening? She wanted to ask her mother, but knew she would gain no reply.

"Derlik!" shouted Faeth as she passed the final few bodies to reach the front. A line of guards blocked her from pressing forward any more.

"Father!" Aerhee shouted.

His disheveled head lifted and gave a small, piteous smile. Dry lips mouthed the words, *"I love you."*

"I love you too," Aerhee said. Her mother couldn't speak as she sobbed.

The Thane of Scholarship stood with a hand raised to silence the crowd.

"Whole is the Holy!" he called.

"Zhaesmen," addressed the Thane, "This *Priessman* will be punished for threatening our Court with Priess ideals and the agenda of the *Bronze Seers*. We will eternally capture his sin as a warning for those who are tempted to replicate such treachery. Whole is the Holy!" He stepped over to address a group of Zhaesmen who stood beside Derlik.

Aerhee didn't know what was happening. *Why would they do this to him? All he ever did was love us?*

A large, hooded man pulled on a thick rope that was attached to the hanging cauldron. Molten metal as viscous as honey poured out and covered Derlik. His cries could only be heard for a second. The liquid metal cooked his skin like an unskinned chicken, sealing him into a metal tomb.

"Da!" Aerhee cried.

Derlik had become a horrific bronze statue. He would be immortalized in the very ore that he mined for in the Cloven Gleff as a vile insult to his attempt to provide for his family. The statue was more reminiscent of an enormous pile of metallic mud with two arms stretching upward. The only detail that remained was an indent where his mouth was, screaming in agony.

The audience gaped at the monstrous creation. There was no need to cheer for the cruel display.

Aerhee's lip started to bleed as she bit into it to muffle her crying.

The Thane of Veneration stood. "This statue will remain at the foot of the Canton of Veneration as a warning to all who oppose Zhaes order and the Patriarchy of Scholars. Reflect upon the statements made here today and warn others of the dire consequences of transgressing Laeih's laws."

The Thanes convened for a moment of quiet discussion, and soon after dispersed to continue their day.

Faeth stood with a numb stare, continuing to hold on to her Aerhee. Once the crowd had dismissed the need to remain in contemplation, Aerhee pulled her mother forward to approach her father's bronze tomb.

"Why?" No one listened to Aerhee's cries. "Why did this happen? Why did we have to come here? This is all because we left home! I want to go home! I want to leave! Ma, why does it hurt so much?"

"Aerhee," she whispered. She embraced Aerhee. "Your father needs our farewell." Aerhee nodded her nestling head against her mother's side, wiping tears across the side of her gown.

They approached the statue, heat still radiating off of the metal.

"Will... will father always be here? I want to stay with him. I don't want him to leave."

"His shell will stay, but he is no longer here."

"What do you mean?" *Hope.*

"Your father has joined Laeih in his eternal halls, a much happier realm than this one."

"How do you know?"

"Laeih has taught us that the saints will join him there; I have never met a more valiant man than your father." she looked down to take in her daughter's reaction. "We will join in our own time, but it is our responsibility to live worthy of such glory."

She knelt at Aerhee's side. "Do not let this taint your view of Court Zhaes. This results from *human* error. These people are guilty of murder. Sinners in the faith do not discredit eternal truth." Aerhee nodded. "You will learn this one day, little one."

Aerhee whispered her first sincere prayer. "Laeih, please help. It hurts. Please."

⁕⁕⁕⁕⁕ ⁕⁕⁕⁕⁕

The Present

Cl. er. 332

I understand it now, Mother, thought Aerhee, as she smiled through teary eyes.

The Patriarchy was not guilty themselves, but only those who executed extreme matters to see righteousness reestablished.

She still believed that they knew her father was innocent, but they had become blinded by prejudice. They had been bigots. It was her duty to make Zhaes a better place, not to continue their legacy of hatred. She had failed to do so so far, but there was still time to change.

Her mother's health declined in the years following her father's death. Her mental stability shook with diminishing hope for justice to prevail in Court Zhaes. She died soon after Aerhee left for the southern regions of Kzhek in pursuit of education. Despite the years of healing, the loss still hurt. It had scarred and would never heal, but she had learned to live with it. She cried, not worried that anyone would see.

Her father had been murdered or *"made an example of the consequences of treasonous behavior."* The sins of a select few could not be blamed on the entire Court. Aerhee held to her Zhaes upbringing not in spite of her father's death, but in honor of the sacrifice that her parents had given to rear her as a Zhaeswoman. Political reasoning did not inspire her to remain, but it was the spiritual aspect of the Zhaes culture that held her through tribulation. She knew Laeih just as she knew her own father. She would remain a Zhaeswoman evermore, but the conflict afoot caused her to wonder once again if the political aspect of Zhaes life had begun again to overshadow its religious base.

This was her purpose. To correct the wrongs of the Zhaesmen. To return the focus of their piety to Laeih, away from the idol of politics and power.

Krall Trhet's visits had diminished, leaving her blind to the conflict abroad. She held onto a hope that an alliance between the Zhaes and Tchoyas Kralls would yield a chance of peace.

CHAPTER THIRTY

LOYALTY OF THE PRODIGY

Yetrik shook as he was pulled from his reverie. He turned with the Zhaes Thanes to look at the door.

"Thane Belik!" A Zhaes guard shouted as he entered the Royss' council chamber in the Canton of Agriculture.

Royss glanced up from the map of Kzhek, which was spread across a great table of bronze and polished pale wood. "Speak, Zhaesman!"

"A messenger informed me that the second wave is weakening and Sleff Gorgers have joined the dissenting forces!"

"Sleff *what*?"

"Sleff Gor–"

"I heard you. You are dismissed, Zhaesman."

The guard left the chamber.

"Well then," said Royss after a shaken sigh. He turned to Yetrik. "Glad that you heard that, Gruthman. It seems it's time to call forth those assets that you secured for me with the Beastlings."

"Royss, you cannot, with a sound mind, send those fiends to battle!" repudiated Thane Leisa.

"I can and will." He approached the exit, not considering her opinion.

"Royss!" she contested and followed him. "This is not about decimating those who do not agree with us! These are human lives!"

He halted, giving her only half of his face to view. "A sinner is not greater than a pest due for extermination. They will learn the inflexibility of the law. Have you already forgotten the statue that stands before the Canton of veneration? It seems that the example made by *The Bronze Transgressor* has become a futile sacrifice."

"How *dare* you!" she shouted and stood to follow.

Royss sneered. "You sound as if you knew who that coward of a Priessman was." He shook his head, turning away from her. "Yetrik, follow me."

Thane Leisa stopped to look at Yetrik, her eyes questioning who he would join. He gave Thane Leisa a sorrowful glare and approached Royss.

"Don't worry about Thane Leisa, Gruthman," Royss remarked. "She doesn't recognize how dire our circumstances have grown. I don't know how the Sleffmen found Gorgers, but I don't want to waste time on speculation."

"What about the Zhaes Gorgers?" asked Yetrik.

"I doubt Taeih was able to recruit more than twenty of them. If we are losing strength in our second wave, the Sleff Gorgers must have outnumbered ours. We captured these kaesan for combat, and I intend to see them appreciated."

Thane Leisa's worries unsettled Yetrik, but he did not want to test Royss. He had seen the extent of the Thane's anger.

He followed Royss to the Canton's lowest level and met the Beastlings in a dim chamber as they ate bread and roasted potatoes.

"Are they ready?" Royss startled Runith from the entrance.

"As ready as an overdue pregnant maid!" Runtih raised a chalice. "Nice to see you again, Sir Yetrik."

"Likewise." Yetrik said.

"Derr, you get Khahak with Jhael. I will get Tooreith." Runith turned to Yetrik. "Yes, Khahak, the second kaesan, told us her name eventually, though she was initially unwilling to talk."

Royss waved them toward the door. "Be swift. Each moment you waste talking causes the death of another Zhaesman."

Runith lost his spirited grin and led the party to the menagerie.

Once they arrived, Runith let out the familiar kaesan call. A twin cry echoed back through the dank chambers. A crack of outside light leaked in through high-barred windows at street level. Flamed torches caused shadows to dance throughout the chamber, revealing the corpses of the kaesan's last feast of live lamb.

"What do you want with them?" Runith unlocked the first cage and entered it, while Jhael and Derr entered the other.

"Go to the central square and join the others who are fighting for our city," Royss instructed. "Don't worry about the enemy soldiers at first. Focus on the Gorgers."

"*Gorgers?*" asked Runith. "On the side of the anti-harvesting rebels?"

"I don't know where they got them, but that is beside the point. Eliminate their Gorgers, *then* focus on the others. Is that clear?"

Runith spoke to the kaesan in a cryptic rhythm. This continued for a minute before he returned his attention to Royss. "We'll take care of it."

"Thank you. We will soon drink to our victory."

Eerie speech continued between the kaesan and Beastlings as they proceeded out through a back opening to the menagerie, which led to the back fields of the Canton.

"Whole is the Holy, Zhaesmen!" Royss said with gusto, saluting them. They returned the salute and shout of the Zhaes Ideal. The Beastlings climbed to ride on the backs of the kaesan, holding onto their antlers as the creatures ran forth on all four limbs like lean bears.

"Laeih be with them," muttered Royss.

"Are the Beastlings joining the battle as well?" asked Yetrik.

Royss nodded. "We cannot let the kaesan roam without a voice to control them. They are dangerous, but with these three, I trust we will only yield victory."

"Should I join them?"

"You're not a Beastling."

"I know, but–"

"As far as I can tell, you're not a soldier. War is fought by civilians and directed by noblemen. Do you wish to be another name lost as a casualty or one remembered in years to come?"

"Well... I guess–"

"Do not guess, commit."

"I want to be remembered."

"Then do not lose wisdom in a zealous desire to become a warrior. You're coming with me to work with the other Thanes. Do not forget that this is a conflict for our honor. Maintain yours, Gruthman."

❦

The central alleyways of Kzhek became narrower as the Beastlings and kaesan approached the square. Runith stopped his kaesan, knowing that they were too large to continue.

"We need to go up and across the buildings," said Jhael. "We can enter the square from above."

"I feared the same thing," said Derr

"Why fear? Approaching the conflict from above will yield us a distinct advantage." said Runith. "They will never suspect an attack from above."

The kaesan were more than simple steeds. They had a mind of their own, one more complex than most creatures. The Beastling's commands were simple directions. The kaesan directed the rest themselves.

The Beastlings directed the kaesan to summit the buildings to reach the skyline. Their long limbs helped them climb the buildings and jump between their gaps with ease.

After less than a minute of climbing, the Beastlings and kaesan were on top of the buildings that surrounded the central square. Runith prompted Tooreith to take a closer, yet crouched, glance over the edge. They were high enough to be disregarded; the antlers of the kaesan would appear as large dead trees to any who looked upward. Khahak crawled to their left with Jhael and Derr holding tight to the fur on her back.

"*What do you see?*" Runith asked in the kaesan tongue. Most animals and beasts spoke with poor diction and had simplistic languages, but the kaesan were as intelligent as a prominent Scholar in the Patriarchy.

"*Many fallen warriors in shimmering armor.*" Said the kaesan. "*Large men engage in combat, one with another, though there are more warriors on one side of the conflict.*" Tooreith's voice would sound like a shriek to anyone else, but to Runith it was a symphony of whispers.

"*Turn for me to see.*" He moved Runith towards the edge, though at a cautious distance.

Bloody and dented armor covered the floor. Less than a third of the Zhaes soldiers remained standing. Dear Gorgers were scattered among each side of the conflict, though more remained standing with the rebels.

Runith stepped back and turned to the others. "*Ready to descend, Beastlings and kaesan?*"

CHAPTER THIRTY-ONE

THE VOICE OF THY BROTHER'S BLOOD CRIETH

"Colrig!" Phenmir shouted.

The Sleffman continued to shout, pumping his fist in the air. The scene seemed dire until the Sleff Gorgers arrived. One Sleff Gorger could take out two Zhaes Gorgers on their own without any weapons, only brute strength. They attacked and dodged their enemies' attacks as quickly as any skirmisher. It was clear that Colrig had been training them for a long time.

"Colrig!"

He turned back to Phenmir. "Yes! Come join me, Thane Stolk. See this young Gorger?" He pointed into the battling crowd. "I have known that Sleffman since his birth. His parents would rejoice to see that he has defeated a Zhaes Gorger and even more guards. I will see that he–"

"Colrig, *look up*!" Phenmir said.

"What are you japing at?"

He jogged to Colrig and pointed up. "The western wall." The shrill warning in Phenmir's tone sobered Colrig's enthusiasm as he traced his eyes to the rooftops.

Two eldritch behemoths with giant antlers pounced across the rooftops and climbed down. Half-collapsed buildings made it easy for the beasts to descend to the ground.

"By Heitt's humility! What is that abomination?" Colrig's exclamation caught the attention of the nearby troopers.

With a banshee's screech, the first creatures' cry caused legions to stumble. As they drew closer, Phenmir noticed a man on its back while the other creature carried two. The Zhaes guards cowered alongside their enemies, while some of the Zhaes Gorgers rejoiced at the sight. Their allies noted their excitement and soon joined in with their cheers.

"See the banner." Phenmir pointed to the highest remaining building. A tattered Zhaes banner hung by a single corner; nevertheless, its emblem was clear and recognizable.

"Perding kaesan?" said Colrig. "Those are creatures from bards' tales!"

"Can you see the Zhaesmen on their backs?"

"Beastlings."

Phenmir nodded. "Must be. I doubt they are domesticated."

"Have any of the Endowers come along?"

"Very few, and they have hidden. Why?"

Colrig turned his focus to Phenmir. "Find them. We need a Beastling."

᠃᠃᠃᠃᠃᠃

Colrig ran to find his commanding officers but feared that they had already been called to the front. He dared not return his gaze to the kaesan and maintained focus on his task amidst the carnage. Their claws shred through soldiers like a rushed butcher.

Gorgers stood at least three heads taller than a large person, but the kaesan stood four times larger than a Gorger. Their claws impaled Sleff Gorgers and tossed them across the square with the ease of a child juggling a stone.

Allegiant soldiers threw the swords of fallen troopers and small spears at the kaesan, but no blade could pierce their thick skin.

The kaesan were smart with their approach, never letting themselves be surrounded, but they remained close enough to kill plenty of soldiers. While the Allegiant focused on the kaesan, the Zhaes Gorgers had more success, pushing back against their Sleff counterparts.

Below Colrig laid a fallen Zhaes trooper, proving that the Allegiant forces had crossed into their opponent's lines. The Allegiant had been in control of the second wave but would soon lose progress if the kaesan continued unimpeded.

Is it the duty of a captain to save himself so that he might guide future forces, or is he bound to serve his men until their demise? *Pious is the Giver.* The words of the Sleff Ideal came to his mind. *Perd you, Heitt,* he thought, reaching down to take the Zhaes sword. *Do not make my sacrifice of self be in vain.*

Phenmir ran faster than he ever had. *They're depending on me.*

He found the congregation of masked children hiding in the rubble of a building in the southwestern sector just beyond the square. Port had tipped him off to their hiding place, having noticed Voln's command to retreat.

"Voln!" Phenmir called, pushing past stones into their burrow of debris. "Voln!"

The boy stood from the group. "What's happening out there? It keeps getting louder and louder!"

"Do you have a Beastling among you?"

"Well, I... I..."

Phenmir knelt beside Voln. He felt like shouting, but didn't have time to waste. He stilled himself, trying to focus on the Chuss Ideal that he too often ignored.

"Voln, we need a Beastling. Have any come with you?"

"I don't know," he admitted.

"You really don't know if there are any? There must be thirty or more of you here." Tension straightened his brow.

"I only know five, maybe six of the Endowers here."

"You are their captain, Voln! It's your duty to know them well."

"Do you know all of your warriors?"

Phenmir smirked and focused on the other Endowers. "Are any of you Beastlings?"

A small girl stood from the far left corner, hair disheveled. Her mask was that of a hawk.

Phenmir approached her with a confident grin. She ran to him, but kept her distance. She seemed interested, but still nervous.

"What is your name, Tchoyaswoman?"

"Golma."

"Golma, can I have your help?"

She nodded. He patted her on the shoulder and supported her with the Tchoyas salute, which she eagerly returned. She took a step closer to Phenmir.

A boy then stood with the mask of a whistling man.

"Are you a Beastling as well?"

The boy nodded, "I'm Dronn, Sir Chussman. I can help too."

"Klen and Cheric bless you two." Phenmir stepped away from the Endowers and beckoned the Beastlings forward. "Voln, continue to keep watch over the Endowers."

"Have you ever spoken to a large beast?" he asked them as they jogged towards the Allegiant troops.

"No," replied Golma.

"I commanded and rode an eldeer once," said Dronn. "He was as tall as a cottage and had to lower his antlers to let me climb onto his back. Ask Golma, it really happened!"

"It did," she added.

"Then I have a challenge for you, and these antlers will be much larger."

I'm fighting to save these children, but I am using them in our war? Phenmir almost stopped at that thought. They'll be safe, we only need them to call the kaesan. They'll be safe. It's a sacrifice for the many. A sacrifice for the many. The same justification that the harvesters use. This is different, is it not? He stopped his thoughts. He had made his choice and so had the Endowers when they joined the march to Kzhek.

Before they turned the last corner to enter the square, he held the Endowers by the shoulders.

"Can I trust you two to be brave and hold strong, even when it seems dangerous?"

His words startled them, but they nodded.

"I need you two to try to speak to these creatures. They are being controlled by Zhaes Beastlings. I don't expect you to gain control, but to disrupt the connection between them and their riders. Can you handle being a distraction?" They nodded again. "I will have two Gorgers assigned to your personal protection. You'll be safe, I'll be sure of it."

Yet another promise built upon hope rather than reality. Cheric protect them. Cheric forgive me.

He kept them close at his sides and ran towards the first Gorgers he could find that were outside of the heat of battle.

The Endowers held onto the hem of his garment. "Sleffmen! Gorgers!" he shouted with a waving arm to capture their attention.

They looked up, furrowing their brows as Phenmir approached with the Endowers.

356 ELEGY OF A FRAGMENTED VINEYARD

"What do you want?" one of them shouted. "We need–"

"I am Phenmir Stolk, Chuss Thane of Harmony!"

"Forgive us, Thane. Colrig told us about you, but we didn't know what you looked like."

"No need to apologize." Phenmir shook his head. "I need the two of you to lead these Endowers to the kaesan." He turned, and the Beastlings stepped closer to the Gorgers. "They are Beastlings. Carry them on your backs, or however you wish, just protect them."

"What–why?"

"They are going to help stop the Beastling controlling the kaesan."

They turned to look at the kaesan, who continued to plow through the Allegiant forces. "That will work?" one of the Gorgers asked.

Phenmir nodded. *I hope so.* "Take them close enough that the kaesan can hear their calls, but far enough away that the kaesan cannot reach them.""That's it?"

"They will take care of the rest," said Phenmir. "*Don't let them get hurt.*"

"If you command it, we will."

Phenmir nodded. "May Heitt and Klen guard you."

The Endowers ran towards the Gorgers, who lifted them to hold on to their backs.

Not knowing which salute would encourage the members of differing Courts, Phenmir felt it appropriate to salute them in the manner most dear to him. Phenmir raised his hands to his chest and made a circle with his fingers and thumbs, giving them the Chuss salute. They returned the respective salutes of their home Courts and departed to follow their order. Though the war had divided much of Facet, the Allegiant had reunited it in a unification of distant allies.

Colrig swung at a Zhaesman who impaled a Chussman before him. Each ally that fell ignited a new flame within. He was fueled with retribution for the fallen.

He parried the Zhaesman's first blow and felt the exhaustion of his enemy's slow strike. Colrig had been a part of the fight for only ten minutes, but this soldier gave the impression that he had been fighting since the start of the second wave.

He took advantage of his opponent's fatigue and kicked him down onto the cobblestone after their swords met for a second time. The kick drained Colrig. Soon he would be just as exhausted as his opponent, but he could not give in. He had to continue. The Allegiant depended on him. The Sleffmen depended on him.

The Zhasman tried to stand, but Colrig dashed forward to finish him off. He plunged the tip of his blade into an exposed gap in his opponent's armor, piercing his left chest. As his left arm plunged forward, his right was exposed to the Zhasman's strike.

His enemy fell with the sword still in his breast. Colrig fell back, holding the stump that remained on his right arm. He had jumped to kill without thinking. Rage blinded him, costing him his arm.

He took a step back as the pain crawled up his nerves, though shock kept it somewhat numb. An ally stepped before him to fight the next Zhaesman. Colrig stumbled back from the front lines.

You perding Kulf! You're responsible for more people than yourself. Thoughts of self-depreciation continued as he fled.

He needed rapid aid and a stop to the blood flow. His head already felt loose, but he was more in shock from the loss of his arm rather than from blood loss. Little time remained before the second factor would overcome the first.

As if a blessing from his god Klen himself, he saw Phenmir attending to the wounds of a Gorger just beyond the southernmost left flank. He pressed his hand firmer on the open vessels of his remaining elbow and ran in an adrenaline-fueled focus.

"Tourniquet!" he shouted.

Phenmir turned to his shout, left the Gorger, and ran towards Colrig. He removed his belt and pulled it tight around what remained of Colrig's arm.

"I'm sorry, Sleffman," Phenmir said as he rushed him to the medical supplies," but this will require more than a belt."

"I figured," hissed Colrig through clenched teeth.

Phenmir pressed a thick cloth to the wound. "Another cauterization." He told his aide. "Go grab the materials."

The aide nodded and ran.

Phenmir continued to press the cloth against Colrig's wound, but their attention was simultaneously averted by a harrowing cry from one of the kaesan.

Dronn, the Beastling boy, held onto his Gorger with arms ringed around his neck. While the Endower hung, the large Sleffman covered his ears to muffle the child's beastcall that would cause pain to even the vilest of creatures in the under realms.

"Any luck, little whistler?" asked the Gorger between Dronn's calls.

"I think it might notice me but—"

The sound of a distorted elk call caught their attention. Golma cried out atop the other Gorger's shoulders. The kaesan closest to her replied to her call with a similar screech.

"That one seemed to do something!" remarked the Gorger, who held Dronn.

"Yes, I think I can match that. Cover your ears again." He nodded and lifted Dronn onto his shoulders.

Dronn screeched with more emotion in his call than in any other previous attempt.

The kaesan replied with a screech and shook as if in pain. Golma called right after him and caused her kaesan to shake just as the other had.

Their calls continued to bombard the kaesan, straining their young vocal cords of all remaining strength. The Zhaes Beastlings called at their steeds to focus their attention, but each kaesan's agitation only grew worse. Each creature was torn between calls from opposing masters, causing them to stumble as an angry drunkard.

The closest kaesan shook like a hound after a rainstorm and clawed at its back, tossing the mounted Beastling from its back. The Endowed fell to the crowd and his mount rampaged forward like a wild boar.

⁕⁕⁕⁕⁕⁕ ⁕⁕⁕⁕⁕⁕

Allegiant soldiers fell to their kaesans' swipes, but the creatures no longer differentiate focused on the Allegiant. The Beastling and Endower calls had set the kaesan into their natural state, causing them to attack Allegiant and Zhaes soldiers alike.

The beasts of nature assaulted the two warring parties, regardless of their political conviction. Policy and pride were tenants of a privileged race, not pieces of nature itself. These people, though they were of the same species, could not bind themselves to overcome their differences of opinion, and found it best to resolve the issues over bloodshed and dominance. From an outside glance, a scholar would take the kaesans' unbiased attack to be a godsent cleansing to punish a civilization so foolish for relying on murder to resolve their problems.

The Allegiant and Zhaesmen were forced into cooperation to kill the kaesan before any man-to-man combat could continue.

Moments after the final Zhaes Gorger was eliminated, the first kaesan collapsed in a lake of its own blood.

After losing its companion, the second beast appeared to surrender its morale as its stance fell to severed ankle tendons. Impaled by an Allegiant Gorger, the spirit of the final kaesan was freed from the battlefield.

The clash continued, continuing the cycle of death until the inevitable rise of the victor. Many Sleff Gorgers remained, having only lost a near-fourth of their numbers against the kaesan.

So it occurred that the Allegiant overcame the Zhaes forces. Neither party was guilty of murder, for they were commanded to kill under the supervision of their superiors. Neither side sought malice nor did they strive for evil. Both sides of any conflict ultimately seek the path that they deem most benevolent in its own nature. Many would become orphans, widows, or widowers after the events of the day, and this would not be the end of such bereavement.

The clashes came to a gradual cease. Soldiers stood at ease and fell in exhaustion. Phenmir heard the trample of boots running towards him in the quieting square. Exhaustive strain diminished the Allegiant's desire for celebration, though very few felt it appropriate to celebrate the death of so many.

"Thane Stolk! Thane Stolk!"

Phenmir gave him his attention with exhaustive hope; his eyes questioned the validity of the soldier's oncoming words. *Is it true, Chussman?*

His ears rang, but the battlefield felt more silent. His heart pounded. He wiped the sweat that fell from his brow and focused on the Chussman.

"No more than five Zhaes guards escaped. It is finished. We have taken central Kzhek."

CHAPTER THIRTY-TWO

IMPERFECT SAINTHOOD

"Our kaesan have what?" Exclaimed Royss, turning to the messenger who stood in the doorway of the Canton of Agriculture's council hall.

"The kaesan have fallen... and the remaining Zhaes guards have either perished or retreated."

Sheath exhaled deeply.

Royss stared at her, but returned his focus to the messenger. "Leave!"

The messenger dashed away.

"Sheath," Royss said with hushed antagonism. "Does it make you happy to see us fail? Does it please you to see our city falling into the hands of these dissenters? Is this what you wanted?"

"I'm not happy to see what is happening to our city, but I am glad to hear that the kaesan have been stopped before they could destroy more of our city."

"You need–"

"No, *Royss*, I will not debate further. We have differences of opinion, but we need to find common ground *now*. I believe your voice to be, on occasion, too liberal with your radical methods. Perhaps I am too conservative in the preservation of life. Can we put this aside before we lose even more?"

He nodded "Forgive me, Sheath. I think we can all benefit from some clear thinking. You want to go forward together. Do you have any ideas?" He turned to the others in the room, Thanes Gromm, Lettre, and Tywing, alongside Sheath and Yetrik.

"Anyone else have an idea of where to go from here? I've exhausted mine" Royss stood with open arms. The council members avoided his gaze, each staring off in contemplation. "Gromm? Do you–"

A knock on the door captured the council's attention. Fheo, the Caser's scribe, entered and took one of the few empty seats at the table. His clothes were dirty and torn.

"I have a message from Caser Kleeh and Krall Trhet of Court Tchoyas."

Everyone's eyes opened wide. Fheo relayed his experiences in Fayis.

"How could Aehree–"

"Stop, Royss," said Sheath. "Let him talk."

"The Tchoyas Krall does not condone harvesting," explained Fheo, "but he believes that the previous state of Facet was better suited to each Court's interests. Complete opposition or support for harvesting is bound to result in massacres, but stopping these rebels might help peace return. Krall Trhet extends his hand in an offer of desperation. I am sure his proposal has certain conditions, but we cannot know their extent unless you come to Fayis. Seeing the state of the city, it seems like you all could use his refuge."

"Come to Fayis?" scoffed Thane Gromm.

"Where else would you go?" asked Yetrik.

Royss smiled at him. "You think we should go, Gruthman?"

"The other Thanes have been captured by the rebels," said Thane Lettre. "We need to leave before we join them."

"Why not go to Gruth or Priess?" asked Thane Gromm.

"Too much of a risk right now," said Thane Lettre. "Tchoyas is closer and is a sure way to strike at the heart of the rebels. Turning one of their Courts to our side is an invaluable offer."

"Sheath?" asked Royss. "What do you think?"

"I question the sincerity of Krall Trhet, but I fear we have nowhere else to seek refuge. I am sure Tchoyas will have the resources for us to communicate with Court Gruth and Court Priess for future alliances."

"Are you going to join us, Yetrik?" asked Royss.

"I suppose I have no other option," said Yetrik. "When are we leaving?"

"If you insist on going to Tchoyas, then we must leave immediately," said Thane Gromm. "We do not need to take much. I can see that the brethren of the Tchoyas chapterhouse of the Patriarchy aid our *diplomatic* stay in their Court."

Royss nodded. "Following our leave, I will send messengers to scout the other Cantons to tell the other Thanes that we are heading to Fayis. If the palace remains under our control–."

"They have already captured the palace, Thane Belik." said Fheo. "I witnessed its seizure upon my arrival."

Royss stepped away from the table. "I suppose we have no time to waste. Our Canton can only stand as a target for so long until it is captured. Yetrik and I will prepare the carriage."

Royss gave the Thanes the Zhaes salute and waved for Yetrik to follow him.

Yetrik approached Royss as they left the room. A question burned in his throat. *Am I scared of Royss*? He tried to ignore his anxiety, but could not silence it. Instead, he pushed through.

"Royss?"

The Thane turned to him with a raised eyebrow.

"Do you recall our conversation about... the Middlemen?"

Royss raised his eyebrow, taking interest. "How could I not?"

"I wondered. If Beastlings can communicate with the kaesan, could they speak with the middlemen?"

"We wouldn't have time to find the Beastlings before we leave, *even if they survived*."

"Yes. I understand that, but I know that Krall Trhet works closely with the Tchoyas Endowers. Maybe we can ask for his help when we arrive in Fayis. Maybe even add a Foreteller to the company to guide us on a safe path to the Middlelands."

"Can we be sure that a Beastling, let alone an inexperienced child, can communicate with a Middleman? They are not animals, more plants than humans."

"Is it not worth a try?"

Royss looked at him with a charming grin and chuckled. "I would much rather try to build a radical alliance with them than to join a Priessman. We can discuss this again once we arrive in Fayis. Refine your proposal and we can speak with Krall Trhet."

Yetrik smiled with a forward gaze of self-satisfaction. Royss was far from a perfect exemplar, but he allowed Yetrik to flourish beyond the boundaries of his home Court.

Royss had a way with people. His silver tongue captured enemies and allies alike. Yetrik did not doubt that Royss could sway the Krall in his favor.

They proceeded out through a back passageway, passing the courtyard to reach the stables. Fheo had been an unexpected guest, but the man who sat behind the Canton was an even bigger surprise.

Runith sat slumped against a wall.

"I didn't know where to go," said Runith, coughing and spitting bloody mucus onto the ground.

"You... where are the other two?" asked Royss.

"Dead. In the center. I fell from the kaesan onto a pile of leather-armored bodies, buffering my descent while they had nothing but cobblestone to meet their heads. I guess armor would have been a nice investment."

Yetrik studied Runith's bruised face, bearing a few lacerations compared to the tears on his armament. Though he had escaped, his clothing proved that he had endured a share of man-to-man combat.

"Tywing is with us." Royss extended his arm to help the Beastling stand. "He can patch your injuries. We are leaving for Fayis and *you* are coming with us."

Royss seemed to help the Beastling out of pity for his condition, but Yetrik felt his presence was a divine gift to progress his plan in the Middlelands.

"Tchoyas?" asked Runith. "Are you already surrendering?"

"Far from it."

The past hours felt like a dream to Yetrik. Turning to Runith, he recalled experiences with him and the other Beastlings. He hadn't had an opportunity to mourn the fallen, but a tear fell as he remembered the two other Beastlings. He would never see them again. His small share of grief caused him to tremble at the thought of how Runith must feel. It was not only Runith that would feel the sting of bereavement this day. All Zhaesmen had lost the heart of their homeland.

Royss gathered the carriages and ghete and the company left within an hour of receiving Fheo's message. Their fate, and the future state of their Court, had now been given to rely upon a previous enemy, the Krall of Court Tchoyas.

CHAPTER THIRTY-THREE

ECHOES OF AN ALLY

D ays passed in silence, becoming a span of numb existence. Aerhee saw the rise and fall of the sun but had stopped counting how many days had passed. The beginning of her captivity instilled fear and panic. She had since become apathetic and spent most of her days in slumber and meditation. She thought of what she would do after she was free, but each idea floated away like parchment in a Vestning breeze.

A succession of three knocks, each one hardened by the usage of bare knuckles on the wooden door, pulled her from her reverie. The visitor entered without an invitation.

"Caser, we have arrived," said Fheo.

It pleased her to see a familiar face. *How long has it been? Weeks? Months?*

"I thought I told you we are beyond titles, Fheo."

A grin gave a lift to the right corner of his mouth. "As you request, Aerhee."

"*We*, you said, who else?"

"Thanes Tywing, Lettre, Leisa, Belik, and Gromm." She was relieved to hear that Sheath would join them, but was less so thrilled at the presence of the latter two. "As well as Runith the Beastling."

"Has Krall Trhet permitted my parole?"

"I believe so. We arrived less than an hour ago and he wishes to consult with us."

"Very well, but I–"

"Krall Trhet has already ordered for his servants to bring you a change of clothes."

"Thank you, Fheo.""We will be in the throne room when you are ready." He shut the door.

She had not expected to feel such joy from seeing him, but her appreciation for minute pleasures had grown. She did not wish to repeat her captivity, but she felt it was an advantageous time for introspection.

Her new clothing arrived—with long sleeves and a high collar fit for a Zhaeswoman—and she soon after departed to meet her kin of Court Zhaes.

The Zhaes nobility stood in an intimate circle as Aerhee arrived before the doors of the throne room. An unfamiliar face stood among the revered Thanes, that of a young Gruthman whom she did not recognize.

Sheath turned out from their group and invited Aerhee forward with a welcoming smile.

"Who is the Gruthman?" She asked.

Royss stepped closer to her. "This is Yetrik. He has served as a diplomat and adviser to our Court in a dire time of need."

"I do not recall any Gruth Thane named Yetrik."

"I'm not a Thane, Caser Kleeh but —"

"Not *yet*," answered Royss with his arm on the Gruthman's shoulder, "but he was sent by Thane Gett on a special order. He was one of the 'Gruth messengers' we spoke of before your departure. Along with our Beastlings, he aided in the capture of two kaesan!"

"Kaesan? So you followed through with *that* tactic?" Their party took time to recount the events of the invasion of Kzhek up until their arrival in Fayis as they awaited the Krall. He was relieved that none of them condemned her for fleeing to Tchoyas. She expected Sheath to understand, but neither Gromm nor Royss made mention of it. *Do old disagreements die when people are forced to collaborate?*

Though she kept her composure, she could not feel as if she were learning of the death of a loved one. Her city had fallen at the cost Zhaes pride. *Zhaes pride.* Those two words were by definition antonyms but had grown synonymous by their adamant desire for perfection. Would events have occurred differently if they heeded her call for an armistice? She knew her efforts yielded no peace, but she now felt that the initial hope was futile, seeing how easily Krall Trhet was persuaded to join their cause. The Krall of Court Tchoyas, the Court whose Ideal was unfaltering loyalty, had betrayed his previous allies for his gain. She had heard rumors of people disliking the Krall. Now she could see why. *This must not be the first instance of acting against what he preaches. Can we trust him? Should we? Have all the Courts of Facet begun to denounce their Ideals and pursue their own selfish desires?*

The throne room's doors opened and an ox mask stared at them through the cracks. "He is ready for you."

Thane Tywing stepped forward to open the doors and lead the group into the Krall's capacious throne room.

"Heloath, Zhaesmen. I am glad to see that you arrived safely." The Krall spoke from atop his throne. The chamber walls allowed for an echo that made one feel as if he talked beside them.

Royss stepped before the party. "Might I ask how you wish to aid our cause?"

"Direct, I see. Very well. As your messenger should have informed you, I long for the peaceful state in which we dwelt only earlier in this year. The Sleffman by the name of Colrig, the very same who slew the late Chuss Krall, visited my Court before the attack on your capital. Oh, how I wish he had not set such conflict in motion. I may *struggle to accept* the harvest in my Court, but I have no right to condemn the acts of others in their respective lands."

Royss nodded and stepped closer to the base of the staircase. "I too wish to see the return of autonomy to the Courts, Your Grace. How are we to verify your loyalty to this cause so soon after you pledged loyalty to our enemy? Is this not a betrayal?"

"Is it easy to reject conformity when pressured between two armies? It seems that you have likewise faced the force of their *intimidation*. The definition of my Ideal is beyond your jurisdiction. I did not have the power to oppose my Thanes. As a Thane yourself, you know how little power your Krall actually has when compared to the Thanes when they are united. Now that some of my Thanes are away with these rebels, *I* command the Court."

"And what about your other Thanes?" asked Royss. "The ones who are still here in Fayis?"

"They will comply. I will see to that."

Aerhee scowled, staring into the eyeholes of the Krall's mask.

"No need for any more arguments," the Krall continued. "You will see my loyalty proven soon enough. Tell me, Zhaesmen, what would you request of me in order to see your goal achieved?"

"We need an envoy sent to Courts Gruth and Priess." Royss replied. "With aid from these pro-harvesting Courts, we can reestablish our authority in our home Court. Aside from this, Yetrik will require two of your Endowers for a southern caravan to the Middlelands."

The Krall leaned forward, squinted eyes visible through his mask slits. "*My* Endowers?"

"Yes, Your Grace. I have been informed that the organization of your Endower force is most remarkable. You are fortunate to have so many survive their neonatal years."

"What would you have with them? You Zhaesmen should know that they are far less experienced than any Endowed. Is this not the very reason for which you harvest? To utilize adults when children are 'too young' to know how to wield these powers?"

"I agree, but we have no immediate access to any Endowed outside of the few in our company. The Endowers will suffice for this task. We don't need them in battle, we just need their abilities. I have heard great things about your *trained* Endowers."

"Which Endowers?"

"A Beastling and a Foreteller."

"Why these two? Why the Middlelands?"

"Our trust is yet to be given, Your Grace. Perhaps once you earn it, we can discuss the intricacies of our machinations, as you have suggested. Do not let the other Endowers know about our request."

The Krall eased back into the base of his throne. "Very well, though I should have you known that some of my Endowers have joined the conflict in Kzhek."

"We can worry about those children later. For now, we thank you, Your Grace, for your compliance and discretion. Once we see that an alliance is bound between our Courts, we will be more willing to divulge the most intimate of plans. This is merely the beginning of a long road."

"I agree. We have much more to discuss, Thanes of Court Zhaes, but you deserve some rest." the Krall looked down upon one of the guards at the base of his throne's stairs. "Take these Zhaesmen to their quarters for the evening." The guard nodded and proceeded towards the door to the throne room.

The Krall turned back to his guests. "I will have a caravan provided for Priess to leave on the morrow. Yes, I recognize that this is early, but it is best not to delay. I can see that you have the second caravan to Gruth following success in Priess. Do you have any other needs before the conclusion of this day?"

"That will be all for now, Your Grace." Royss bowed and followed the Krall's guard away out of the room.

Sheath stepped to Aerhee's side as they departed. "Aerhee, have you fared well during your stay in Tchoyas?"

Sheath knew Aerhee to not be easily humored, but the Caser gave into a pitiful chuckle.

"How would you feel to be imprisoned when seeking peace?" She calmed herself with an airy sigh. "I suppose many have been in worse conditions. My holding quarters were closer to the Krall's personal chambers than to a dungeon."

"How long did he keep you in there?"

"It began only days after I was last seen at the council. How long that has been, weeks or months, I cannot say."

Sheath nodded. "And the Krall? What did you think of him? Surely you have spoken."

"Not as much as you would presume. I have a feeling that he is a reclusive ruler. He was polite enough to provide for my means and was reasonable with my care, but he seems to have more working behind his mask than he shows."

"When have you ever met a politician that does not harbor some secret?"

Aerhee shrugged. "My time here has given me the opportunity to think."

"How so?"

"I have not taken time to live beyond my office as of late."

"As of late? Aerhee, when have you taken time for yourself?"

Aerhee let out a nervous laugh. "I'm still influenced by my upbringing. I thought about it, you know? The death of my father. It remained a dark shadow, but I now feel more appreciative of his efforts. He stood by his convictions despite his accusations. You've read my memories. You know how it all happened. He gave everything, even his life, to give me one worth living. My appreciation was hidden behind my hatred of the Pat–" she looked at Thane Gromm who walked ahead of them. "Hatred of injustice, but I... I feel like I can let it go."

Sheath looked at her friend as if she were a stranger. "You do not need to forget the wrongs done to your family. Those Thanes acted outside of the Zhaes law."

"I know, and that's not what I mean. I can recognize their errors and improve myself because of it. There is more to righteousness than solely following the law. It is about one's character and pursuing beneficence for all men and women. I think that is my purpose in all of this, to preserve the heart of our Zhaes faith while the whims of humankind aims to distort it."

"You speak as a Chusswoman."

"Jest as you will, but affection is something I have neglected for a long while. Zeir knows more than any other."

Sheath smiled at her resolve. "I'm sure he would appreciate that. That man has a soul more enduring than any Gruthman."

"Have you ever wondered if harvesting is worth the price of warfare? Death in exchange for more death under the justification of a *higher society*? This has become a game of deciding who should perish for the state of our desired society. Am I mistaken?"

"It is well that this was not spoken to Royss," Sheath whispered. "He would not stand for such treasonous words."

"I do not insist on treason. I only propose a question. If two men insist on burning each other's possessions, when does one capitulate in order to preserve what little remains?"

"All sin begins with a chain of gradual justifications. Be careful with your doubts."

"I will harbor them until they are resolved."

"Maintain trust in the society that has built you. There is rationality to our methods." She smiled with slight admiration and lingering sorrow, leaving Aerhee to step beside Thane Tywing for an inquiry.

Remaining at least three paces behind the procession, Aerhee kept to herself and reflected upon her exchange. *I was built on principles of loyalty to one's kindred people, not by the admiration of law. If anyone was acting by means of treason, it would be unjust rulers as they discard the lives of their underlings for their gain.*

With a feigned, pleasant visage, Aerhee recalled upon the words spoken by those who she thought to be her enemies, finding some truth in their intentions.

Care is the creed.

CHAPTER THIRTY-FOUR

KAMEN

"Have they been located?" Phenmir asked as Port entered the grand hall of the palace of Kzhek, now under their control.

Port shook his head. "I'm afraid not, sir. The Canton of Agriculture was the last one we captured. Some Zhaesmen there were willing to cooperate and mentioned seeing the Thane departing on a ghete carriage alongside four or five others."

Phenmir nodded. "But the other Cantons are..."

"Under our control, sir. While we have captured some of the Thanes, it seems that the Thanes of Agriculture, Diplomacy, Haleness, and Veneration have fled."

"I'll have a scouting party leave within the hour."

Port approached Phenmir with four cautious steps. "Excuse my optimism, but can't we rejoice, sir? As you inferred, these rogue Thanes will be captured, but we have the other Thanes and the Krall under our finger. Kzhek is the Allegiant's... for now."

He arose to accompany Port out of the chamber. "Yes, but that does not diminish our responsibility. Find our Thanes and other leaders within the palace. Have them meet me in the dining hall. I will find Colrig to lead us in a meeting to discuss the next steps forward." Port nodded. "I expect you to be among us, Sleffman. You are as much a leader as any Thane."

Port bore a shy smile and descended the staircase before him as Phenmir remained to look over the balcony of the second level.

Within mere hours, the tide had turned in their favor at the mercy of Cheric's timing of Colrig's arrival. Colrig had Phenmir work as an adviser on the battlefield, but he would now have to take the office of a bureaucrat, placing his men like game pieces to maintain power.

What does the possession of Zhaes entail? Can we keep it? Do we have it? Will Colrig insist on usurping the Krall to initiate a change in harvesting policy? What of the Zhaes loyalists? How many... His mind raced like a Ghete antagonized by a reflected sunbeam. Worries clouded his assignment. His mind had been so fixated on the capture of Kzhek. Had he believed that they could ever make it to this point? Colrig had, and he had to borrow some of the Sleffman's hope.

⟡⟡⟡⟡⟡ ⟡⟡⟡⟡⟡

Thane Trhet–the Tchoyas Krall's granddaughter–closed the door, entering as the final attendee of their table-side council, marking the first gathering since the victory in Kzhek's center.

Phenmir turned his head to the south end of the table, making eye contact with Colrig to initiate the discussion. Colrig remained lackadaisical and stared at Phenmir without any rise, as if he were saying, *"You have the floor, Chussman!"* Phenmir knew that his office as high advisor would only become more cumbersome as the Harmony Allegiant spread.

Phenmir rose and adjusted his tunic. "Chussmen, Tchoyasmen, Sleff-men, our first triumph has come." Cheers erupted with banging on the table and clapping hands. Phenmir smiled but lifted a hand to continue speaking. "The *first*, we must recognize, does not signify the overturning of harvesting. We have more dignitaries to persuade and more alliances to forge before all of Facet can agree on ending the harvest."

Nods and civil smiles decorated the faces of the council members as hands rose before Phenmir fell back into his seat.

"Might I offer a suggestion, Thane Stolk?" Asked Thane Trhet. He replied with a nod and she spoke. "I value the contribution of our Sleff allies, but what about the rest of their Court? We may coerce the powers of Gruthmen to eventually join us, but I find it a fallacy to prolong the procurement of the rest of Court Sleff."

Colrig bit his lip. "I would be a poor kulf of a leader if I had not thought about my people. Yes, Thane Trhet, it would benefit us to have the entirety of my Court on our side, but we cannot overlook the state of the people. You all know that the Sleff economy is suffering. I know this more than any of you, but if we focus on my Court now, we will only drain their resources. Capturing Gruth would ensure that we have a hold in the agricultural epicenter of Facet. We may not need the textile and arts that Priess has to offer, but they will provide more than Sleff at this time. We need to stabilize our hold here and in the other Courts first. Taking Sleff will cost us more than we would gain."

Thane rested against the back of her chair with a sigh.

Thane Holmn leaned forward, staring at the others through her fanged mask. "I agree with Colrig. Court Gruth would be an invaluable resource, but we well know how they will perceive our attack on Kzhek. If I were a Gruthwoman in favor of harvesting, I would expect my Court to be the next target after the fall of Kzhek. I would not be surprised to learn that the missing Thanes have fled to Thusk to incite the Gruth nobility to prepare for that very danger. With the losses that we have already faced, we need to rest and reinforce our army before another conquest. Our efforts would be best spent ensuring our control in this city and in strengthening Chuss and Tchoyas. As the enemy inevitably grows, we could lose our home Courts, besides Sleff, without preventative maneuvers."

Colrig thanked her with the Tchoyas salute.

"How do you propose we secure our control in Kzhek?" Phenmir asked.

"We will have to divide our power in order to strengthen our pillars," said Colrig. "Some of you will be sent to fortify Chuss and Tchoyas, but most of us should remain here as Kzhek recovers."

"What about the Endowers?" Voln asked. "Do you want us to return to Tchoyas?"

"We can send some of you with the returning Thanes," said Phenmir, "but I would like *your* aid with me here, Voln. I will appoint worthy Chussmen to return to my Court, work the rejectionists as a bridge to their Zhaes brethren and sisters."

"You cannot remain here, Phenmir." Colrig's rebuttal took him by surprise. "Your Court needs you, Thane. If you want to fulfill your role as the Thane of Harmony, you need to establish your presence in your Court, not abroad. Do you not recall how we left them?"

Phenmir looked at his palms on the table as he reorganized his thoughts. "Very well," he nodded.

Colrig offered him the Chuss salute.

How had he disregarded returning to his home in Sliin? Perhaps the idea has crossed through his thoughts, though it had passed like a Krall through the city center, noticeable yet untouchable. His anxiety about maintaining the integrity of the Court was overshadowed by his longing to reunite with his wife and son. He was too preoccupied with his crusade to write to them. Had Sliin organized itself since the anarchy following the Krall's assassination?

They were victorious. He survived to see his family. *Cheric, I thank–.* He felt disloyal to once again believe in his god now that things had turned in his favor. *Forgive me for doubting thee.* His loyalty to his god could not be conditional. *I pledge to thee my devotion. I am with thee, and forever will be.* Warmth filled his chest. *But please let us see this victory through.*

"... and attend to the structural status of the central square," Colrig said, turning over his shoulder as he noticed Port raising his hand. "Please, Sleffman."

"Sir, I understand your concerns, but we cannot abandon the asset of acquiring another Court, peculiarly *our* Court. Foremost, the Sleffmen are in dire need of our intervention. You say that they have nothing to give us, but this is about helping all of Facet, not only the Harmony Allegiant. The longer we wait, the more they suffer. If we leave Court Sleff to rot, the enemy will take it as an easy victory to add yet another Court to their cause. This *war* was never about control and power, but overturning the oppression of the weak throughout all of Facet."

"Power is a necessary element, no matter how you approach this, Port." Colrig exhibited a slight degree of cautious superiority.

"Power is your concern? Very well then. How is power obtained? Through coercion. Do you expect to gain the Gruth or Priess with two and a half Courts in your possession? Zhaes will rise to power, but we still need time here. Sleff may not amount to much, but it is another title to add to our claim. If you, as a Sleffman, fight for other Courts without control of your own Court, you will be met with laughter rather than a hand of fellowship. If you do not care about the state of *our* people, Colrig, I plead you recognize that there is a value beyond the economic state of a people."

Colrig leaned forward, but let a merryman's grin split his composure. "Port, it appears that these past months have made something of you. You speak with wisdom, boy! No, no *boy* speaks to his superiors with such conviction! You speak with wisdom, *sir*!"

A relieved smile decompressed Port. Colrig bade him forward, placing a hand on his shoulder.

"*This* is the attitude that will gain us the support of Facet! I have expressed my discord with the capture of Sleff, but Port inspires me to reconsider otherwise. I am but a man, and I am worth no more than any of you. Be pleased that I am no Priessman, or those humble words would have never escaped these lips. What are we to do, then? Has Port persuaded us to seek the poor man's land? I am permitted to say that as a born Sleffman, such words of derision from the mouth of a Chussman will earn the strike of my hand."

Silence arose, though no tension was felt as the council considered Port's offer. Some whispered, but Colrig did not seem to mind as he leaned back into his chair.

Phenmir inhaled and caught the attention of the others as he raised his hand. "I agree with Port. With the value that you have brought from your Court, even without the Gorgers, only a fool would believe that there is nothing else of value for us there. If we wait much longer, the Sleff rejectionists will either join our enemy or fall victim to their path to conquering."

"Is that what we desire then, Allegiant brothers and sisters?" asked Colrig. "Fortify Zhaes and Chuss while we secure Sleff for our cause?"

"And Court Tchoyas?" Port inquired.

"Fayis *could* use some assistance, but Krall Trhet is already overseeing the progression of our cause. Especially as an anti-harvesting Court, I am sure we have little to worry about, as many of our Allegiant remained in Fayis as we left for Kzhek. I would say the same of Court Chuss, but they lack stable nobility without a Krall. Am I wrong to reserve our numbers for these three Courts, rather than sending some to Fayis, Tchoyas Thanes?"

They shook their heads, though Thane Holmn moved with slight reservation. Phenmir noted her hesitation and attributed it to his own worries over Krall Trhet's rule. Something was amiss with that man.

Colrig stood, placing hands on his hips. "So it shall be! Port, you have earned advancement with your valor. Port will lead our forces to obtain the seat of power in Court Sleff as *Thane* Port Kamen, the new Sleff Ment of Harmony."

INTERLUDE IV

Bashin sat on a staircase. It was not the staircase in the Canton of Veneration to which he delivered a prisoner. It was the staircase leading into, or what remained thereof, the Canton of Endowment. Kzhek had fallen.

Moans of injuries and mourning came from Chussmen, Tchoyasmen, Sleffmen, and Zhaesmen alike. Patrolmen dressed in yellow and crimson walked over the corpses of Zhaes guards and Gorgers. Bloodied Zhaesmen wore hopeful grins, despite the ruinous square and their fallen comrades. It was obvious who the rebels were among the Zhaesmen.

"Everything well, Zhaesmen?" A tall Sleffwoman asked as she approached Bashin. A dark streak of crusted blood ran down the side of her face.

"As well as one can be with his home in ruin."

She sat and coughed into the crux of her arm. "You look nearly untouched besides some dust. You must have been one of the lucky ones."

"One of the curious imbeciles to wander here after the battle's conclusion."

She inspected him from head to toe. "I assumed so. You did not strike me as a warrior, anyway. What brought you here?"

"So I didn't come to the safest place?" he laughed and spit. "I was in the Canton of Veneration when this all happened. Your people kept me there until you were 'victorious.' I suppose we are under your control now? Zhaes has fallen."

"If you are here, I assume you are part of the opposition?"

Bashin shrugged. "I am here to observe. I am a Zhaesman and will remain one until I meet Laeih in the life beyond."

Her brows furrowed with a squint.

He laughed. "I will be whatever my people wish me to be, for or against. What am I but a brick in the city's wall? What would *you* want of me, Sleffwoman?" *Would you have me dead for the Endowed that I am?*

"I would have you as an ally. I would have every Zhaesman as an ally."

"You want me to plead your cause? Oppose my people?"

"Harvesting is not tied to any nation, merely a choice made by your leaders. Now that your nobility is captive to our alliance, the oppressed voices of the Zhaes Endowers, those alive and dead at your hands, can be heard."

"That is a bold dream, Sleffwoman."

"A dream that is being actualized." She gestured to the square. "What do you say, Zhaesman?"

"Me? Become a dissenter?" he laughed.

She shrugged. "The once dissenters are becoming the new loyalists. Adapt to truth or fall with old allegiances."

I was treated as a tool. A mere convenience for the nobility. Bashin chuckled, shaking his head. *They have already taken the city. What is there to lose? Perd me, I'm rebelling against my very identity.*

He stood. "I'm not joining anyone. I am just here to observe."

CHAPTER THIRTY-FIVE

A BLUE PLEDGE

Yetrik waved as he watched Thanes Tywing and Leisa leave in a carriage for Court Priess. Two Tchoyasmen had joined them on the diplomatic expedition. He wondered when he would see them again.

Yetrik did not dislike the other Thanes, but he had developed a kinship with Royss and Thane Leisa. Royss the unpredictable, yet charismatic leader, while Thane Leisa offered sound direction and the affection of a mother. He wondered how they would fare without Thane Leisa's balancing force in their party.

Hours after the carriage left, the Krall requested their presence at the foot of his throne.

For a brief while, they reviewed the fall of Kzhek as Krall Trhet revealed his insights to the Allegiant's schemes.

Krall Trhet descended the stairs below his throne. He spoke with a subservient tone, one rarely heard from a Krall. "Tonight I will host a feast of unity, where I will display loyalty previously unheard of by even the highest Tchoyas saint. I expect *all* of you to join."

Yetrik approached Royss as they left another one of the Krall's brief meetings. "What was that about?"

Royss raised his brow and folded his arms. "I suppose we shall find out soon. Many take Krall Trhet for an odd and secretive man, but it makes me like him even more."

"Does it bother you at all, the Krall's timing?"

"What do you mean?" asked Royss.

"Every time the Krall calls us to meet, it lasts for five minutes. Why not just send a messenger if he does not want any prolonged meetings?"

"I've wondered as well, but he seems to be reclusive and old enough that his health may be in decline. I am sure the thrill of power and authority grows tiresome and lackluster in the passing of years. If I were in his position, I would abdicate the throne and live out my days in a secluded hamlet."

Royss never seemed the type to grow tired of receiving attention. Yetrik brushed off his concerns and followed the others towards their personal chambers.

The Tchoyasmen who served them treated their company with respect to an obsequious degree. Food was prepared for them three times a day, more if they requested, and they were never left with an unfulfilled request. Yetrik had been given access to the palace's library and found himself once again enticed by a foreign religion. An ache of guilt still bothered him for not researching Laeih while in Zhaes, but he did not doubt that he would revisit Kzhek. Peace would soon return to Kzhek. He was sure of it. At least Royss seemed confident that it would. Doubt and anxiety crept into the corners of his mind like unwelcome imps. Focusing on theology provided an escape.

Klen, the god of Tchoyas, was depicted similarly to the artwork of Laeih and bore alternative resemblances to his god, Deilf. A collection of priestly writings from the ninety-fourth year in the Clerical Era suggested that Klen saw all of his devotees as one of equal value and trusted his authority to the king no more than to the vilest criminal. Earlier texts did not speak of mask use among Tchoyasmen, causing him to wonder when they had implemented it as a core part of Tchoyas culture. Their system of trust seemed ironic compared to the secret hidden behind their bound masks. Their breeding pools had grown together so closely that all Tchoyasmen appeared the same and only differentiated by the carved images that covered their faces.

Yetrik lost himself in study and had forgotten his need to prepare for their upcoming expedition to the Middlelands. Royss had worked with members of the Tchoyas Canton of Agriculture to ensure that they would receive proper sustenance while away. Rumors regarding the Middlemen were not hard to find, but each one was as true as a hunter's claim to have wrestled a banshee. No one knew exactly where in the Middlelands the people lived, nor did they know what food would be available, so such precautions were made in preparation.

They would use a ghete carriage fit for extensive diplomatic tours rather than for brief noble visits. These models were made to last through a variety of terrains and weather patterns. Additional alterations were made to insulate the inner walls if they need to rely upon it for their shelter. Yetrik would not deny his worry over the weeks or months ahead, but was thrilled to see his childhood wonders manifest as militaristic exploration.

He set his books aside and left his room, noticing Royss's door ajar. He wiped his face and scratched his scalp from fatigue, entering the neighboring room to see Royss adjusting a collar on newly adorned noble wears.

"Excuse my informal attire, Thane Belik." Yetrik offered a sarcastic bow.

"Mock all you wish, but dressing like *that* will only attract the most rural of farmhands."

"You were the one who said that you wished to retire in a hidden hamlet."

Royss shook his head, tucking in the frontmost part of his shirt and fastening the highest button. "Are you going to —"

"Yes, I will change soon enough..." Yetrik recognized the golden glow of the setting sun that peaked out from a thin fog. *Was it already time for the feast? Hours pass like seconds while reading.* He left to change into a courtly attire. He finished with hair disheveled, then jogged to meet the others.

Royss did not seem one to care for his appearance with the meticulous care of most nobles, but he was the last to arrive at the west doors to the dining hall. Banter echoed beyond the doors.

"My stomach feels as if it has digested itself, you kulf!" exclaimed Runith as Royss approached their company.

"Perd you. You could benefit from losing a little weight," Royss responded. Runith's lips lifted into a chuckling grin.

Thane Lettre bore an uncomfortable smile, as if he were witnessing a performance of a naked merryman. Harsh language was a rarity among the Zhaes, especially among those who were believed to be the most pious members of their Court. Yetrik didn't mind hearing the cursing, but did not like to curse himself. The more he interacted with Zhaesmen, the more he understood that very few lived according to the righteous law that they professed.

Thane Lettre motioned to the door, aiming to brush off the crude jesting between Runith and Royss. The company nodded in unison and Runith opened the door.

The hall was filled with candelabra and chandeliers that reflected the shimmering light. A large gray table with a metallic lining stretched long enough to seat twenty people. The Krall sat by those who seemed to be some of his Thanes. It was not a large group, yet the occasion impressed Yetrik.

Krall Trhet's page, a boy in his late teens, guided them to their respective seats. Yetrik sat on the Krall's left side with two children between him and the cathedra, each one with an expressionless guard at the back of their seat. The guards were armed with double-ended spears that were more like a blade rather than a standard spear. Although Yetrik felt slight discomfort from their daunting presence, he was pleased that the children were the only two backed by guards.

Before taking his seat, Royss took no notice of the guards and placed a hand on the backs of their seats. "Who might be our young and dignified guests, Your Grace?"

"You requested two Endowers to accompany you to the Middlelands." replied the Krall. "This is Shaera, a Beastling." The girl in the quail mask gave a timid smile through the open beak of her carved face. "To her left is Blenn, your Foreteller. I felt this was an appropriate time to acquaint yourself with your traveling companions." The boy wore the mask of an open mouth with a tongue to each side, each tongue traced up to touch the outer aspect of his eye holes. Reacting more enthusiastically than the girl, he sat with a defined posture and gave Royss the Zhaes salute, proud that he knew it.

Royss smirked and returned it with a humble bow. He turned his gaze up to the other attendees. "Seeing their silver mask accents, I assume these are your Thanes, but it seems some are missing. I particularly remember your granddaughter and do not see her here."

The Krall leaned forward to speak across the children to Royss, who was now seated. "If you recall, I said that some of my Thanes were a part of the crusade on your Court."

"Ah, yes," Royss nodded.

"I have spoken with *these* Thanes," the Krall gestured to them, "to ensure a dignified meeting free of contention. They know that you are here to help us find peace between our Courts. With us are the Thanes of Diplomacy, Scholarship, Utilities, and Agriculture. I am sure you will meet my Thanes of Endowment, Veneration, and Progress in due time."

Yetrik stared across, seeing contemptuous eyes through many of the Tchoyas Thanes' eyeholes. Though some of their masks depicted joyful faces, they hid the anger beneath. *How does the Krall hope to join us when his Thanes oppose our cause?*

Krall Trhet arose. "Shall we begin?" The Zhaes company nodded, but the Tchoyasmen kept still. "Heloath Zhaesmen and fellow Tchoyasmen. Thank you for joining us this evening. May our gods guide us to see this war brought to a swift end."

He took his seat and raised a glass of violet wine and drank it.

The feast consisted of multiple small courses that sampled the most renowned of Tchoyas delicacies. Yetrik loved the variety of western tastes, which proved much better than the Gruth imitations of their style. The Zhaesmen ate at a slower pace, though he could not tell if it was out of politeness or a dislike of foreign taste. Pondering upon it, he recognized that this meal relieved his gustatory lusts from lack of spice in Zhaes cuisine. The Tchoyas potatoes were roasted with pine and topped with a piece of soft white cheese. Zhaes potatoes were boiled and were often undercooked.

The feast continued on for eight courses, and more for Runith and Royss, who did not seem opposed to Tchoyas cuisine.

Yetrik expected that the meal had ended, but considered otherwise as two guards entered through each door and stood in front of them as they shut all entryways to the feast hall.

Yetrik turned to Royss with an inquisitive eye but found him shrugging off any curiosity as he took a fist-sized bite from a pork thigh. Caser Kleeh and Thane Lettre were engaged in conversation about the effort put into cooking the first course, which apparently required an entire week of preparation from no less than ten qualified cooks.

Dismissing Royss' lackadaisical attitude and the inattentiveness of the others, Yetrik turned to the right to see if Krall Trhet took note of guards who had entered. His head turned in slight observance with minimal movement. The Krall straightened his posture.

The Krall finished the remaining sip of wine and beckoned his page to fetch him more. While he waited, he placed his hand on the back of the seat to his left, turning to speak in a hushed tone to the guards. The guards then spoke to the Endowers, inviting them to stand after wiping their mouths and hands clean of food residue.

"You must excuse these two for the evening," the Krall motioned to the Endowers as they removed themselves from the table. "I have asked that they receive ample rest as they prepare for your departure."

They bid a polite farewell as the children left. Two days still remained until their departure to the Middlelands, but Yetrik did not want to debate with the Krall. He ignored it and continued to finish his final course.

After Runith refused another plate, servers brought each of them a small piece of cake to cleanse their pallets with a light sweet. The servers called it "zupan-tae," which was apparently an old traditional sweet given to enemies to make amends. Yetrik took his first bite, savoring the mild sweetness of the purple yams baked into the flour. Honey and butter were browned over heat, then folded into the dough for baking. A light cream with was spread across the top in a swirl. He had forgotten the bliss of sweet baking, having become accustomed to Zhaes baking that never used more than a drop of honey.

"Fret not," spoke Krall Trhet as he took another nonchalant bite from his cake.

"Over what?" Caser Kleeh asked. She looked at the Tchoyas Thanes who were coughing, seemingly struggling to clear their throats. Their coughs became more violent as each one of them joined in a fit, yet no Zhaesman was affected.

"Krall... I mean Your Grace." Yetrik asked, "are you not concerned about your Thanes? Something is wrong."

Distraught shouts had started to echo throughout the chamber. The Tchoyas Thanes continued to fight for breath and the Zhaesmen stood and shouted.

"He can't breathe!"

"Somebody, help!"

"Guards! Quick!"

The Thanes gradually fell from their chairs, now convulsing with their eyes rolled back. Krall Trhet continued to take small bites from his zupan-tae.

"As I stated, *fret not* and *observe*." The Krall's tone turned into a command, like an exasperated parent directing their child.

Royss walked over to the Krall with clenched fists. "Your Grace, is this your doing?"

Krall Trhet nodded with eyes fixed on his plate.

"Did... did you poison them?" asked Thane Lettre.

Krall Trhet gestured to his fallen Thanes with an open palm. "Observe."

Caser Kleeh shouted for someone to intervene, but she was met by a guard's hand on her shoulder, pressing her back into her seat.

"How else was I to gain sovereignty over these radicals?" said the Krall. "I assure you, they had no intention of progressing *our* goal."

Recognition matched by dread filled Yetrik's mind. Blue-tinged mouths were visible through the masks of fallen Tchoyasmen.

Most of the Zhaes Thanes remained silent, aiming to contemplate the event that had just occurred. No one wanted to risk receiving a similar fate from the Krall. Caser Kleeh muffled her sobs behind her sleeves. Yetrik did not know how to react to the macabre scene. Reality felt distant, and he expected to awaken from a ghastly dream. Reality perpetuated. He awaited the reaction of his superiors as he sat numb and thoughtless. *They expect us to trust him?* He turned to Royss, hoping that he would do something.

Krall Trhet wiped the corners of his mouth and organized the silverware before him to indicate his satiety. "I stated previously that I would prove my allegiance." No one dared to interrupt him, each one eager to hear a sound explanation for his massacre, a massacre of his own people.

"My Court has pledged allegiance to those who seek to overturn harvesting. Though I am the Krall, my Thanes sided with the radicals that stole your capital. You have entered a war, not a conflict of interests, but a war of bloodshed and brutality. Merciless killings will continue until a victor rises. I will see that my other three Thanes are taken care of. With these Thanes out of my way," he gestured to the corpses on the floor, "I alone dictate the politics of Court Tchoyas. Those *dissenters* can never convince the entirety of Facet to plead their cause. They will prolong the war while you strive for a restoration of free policy. Am I mistaken?"

Thane Lettre shook his head.

"I will provide all that I possess to return to a warless state. I hope this evening's example is enough to show my persuasion."

Royss extended a hand to the Krall. "Thank you for your devotion in such dire times."

Yetrik felt guilty once again for hoping that Royss would resolve the insanity of the situation. He should have expected that the Thane would only agree with the Krall's extreme display of "loyalty."

Caser Kleeh stepped back from the end of the table, distancing herself as far as she could from Krall Trhet. She departed through the back doors without any indication of her intentions.

CHAPTER THIRTY-SIX

CRIES OF PROPITIATION

L arceny could not be considered a crime under the shade of Krall
  Trhet's massacre. Aerhee left the palace with only the most necessary of her belongings and took one of Krall Trhet's ghete to return to
Kzhek. She would not declare that she acted in all rationality, but she was
unwilling to work beside any Zhaesman who abided by the actions of a
murderous Krall.

The Zhaes Thanes would see her as a traitor, but they were deceived
by their sense of blind obedience. Aerhee had sworn to be the most
valiant servant of Laieh, and this was not a departure from her ways. It
is significant to note the difference between policy and law. Obsequious
servitude to Laeih with continual correction of faults was a tenant of
Zhaes belief. Harvesting was not a principal of their belief system, but
a mere facet of modern society. *A distraction from deity. An idol. I will*

no longer stand for the desecration of the holy Laeih's Court. Help me, my god, to bring righteousness to thy people.

She would no longer comply with those who kill for mass gain. Pondering upon this, she felt a hypocrite in the similarities between the Krall's action and the policy of harvesting. The bitter taste of guilt arose within her at her past pontifications for the need to harvest. She felt as if he saw the murder of a hen for the first time after a lifetime of eating its meat. Sin is easier to permit when conducted behind a curtain of ignorance.

She fled through the city gates. The rainfall was light, no more than an occasional drip from a cracked basin. Her departure was so unforeseen that she overlooked the need for food along the way. She was bloated from the feast. Acid scratched the back of her mouth from running right after eating. She could skip a few meals, but the ghete would require more sustenance to maintain a brisk pace.

⁂

A few weeks remained in the Holdae season until the arrival of Zeemer. Whispers of the lattermost season of the year touched Aerhee as frozen flakes fell from the sky as she passed over the border into Court Zhaes. She had endured a night of sleepless travel, but the sun was hidden behind clouds, obscuring the time of day. She made it to Court Zhaes before reaching a second nightfall, or so the little daylight she saw led her to believe.

She removed her map with cold fingers. It was Tchoyasmade and, therefore, provided details on their side of the border. It would be useful to direct her to Kzhek but did not identify any villages or stops on the Zhaes side of the border. Rather than sleeping on the roadside under the dying branches of a shrub or tree, she determined it would be wiser to risk prolonging her fatigue in search of any inn. She had to make it to

Kzhek as quickly as possible, but reminded herself that she still had to survive the journey.

The sky changed from a dark purple to a pale gray. After what seemed like four hours following the sunrise, Aerhee was relieved to find billows of black smoke rising from the east. Following the smoke signal, though being sure to memorize her point of deviation from the main road, she entered a small village previously unknown to her. The local inhabitants identified it as Ghek but did not blame her for being ignorant of its existence, for it was only found on most rural maps.

She followed the largest smoke stack to a tavern. An experienced traveler learns to recognize that no matter the land or culture, a tavern can always be identified by a welcoming spirit and an alluring scent of mead dancing with seared meat.

Ten people sat inside, eating and drinking with light banter. She assumed them to all be locals due to the poor weather, but was surprised to see that three of the customers were Chussmen and two were Sleffmen. Travelers were not uncommon on the road from Kzhek to Fayis, but Aerhee had no doubt as to why they were here.

She stared at them and approached in humility.

The Zhaesman, and presumed owner, wore an apron with dark stains from hands that held burnt, greasy meat.

"Heloath," she greeted, trying to cast off judgment of his rough appearance. "What is your price for a night? I'll be out before midday tomorrow."

"What brought you here? Sure you don't–"

"I just need a bed."

He scowled, but reverted back to a yellow-toothed smile. "One petiir."

She nodded and handed him the coin. She was thankful that she had some in her purse, never having to pay for her stay in Fayis.

He took a key from beneath the counter and placed her coin in his apron pocket.

"Down the left corridor, the first chamber on the right side. Leave the key on the bed when you leave."

She smiled and retrieved the key, stepping back to pace around the room. The Chussmen and Sleffmen spoke with gusto, laughing without the shame of being noticed. She was not shy, but this felt more like a confrontation with her past and future self. Prideful against newly humbled. Laeih had given her this opportunity, one that she could not shirk.

Their stares collected on her as she approached. Her boots were not tailored for traveling and carried a hard sole that hit the wooden floor like a horse on cobblestone.

"Heloath, gentlemen." She noted that one of the Chussmen was a burly woman and more muscular than any of the men. "And mistress."

A bald Chussman with a mustache that fell off of the edges of his lips faced her. His scowl morphed into a smirk as he offered a hand to shake. "Evening, Zhaeswoman."

She shook his hand. "Are you members of the group that seized Kzhek?"

The bald Chussman returned his attention to Aerhee. "Are you a rejectionist or a loyalist?"

"Neither, but I am no enemy of yours. Who controls Kzhek?"

"Krall Vheen has been deposed by the head of the Allegiant."

"The Allegiant?"

"The Harmony Allegiant. A coalition of Courts Chuss, Tchoyas, and Sleff to overturn the policy of Harvesting throughout Facet."

"So you are members of this 'Harmony Allegiant'?" *It is too far to turn away. You've found them. Now proceed.*

"Indeed." His hand fell to the hilt on his right hip.

She forced a smile. "I need to speak with the leader of your coalition. I've met him before, a Chussman."

"Thane Stolk?" asked the Sleffman. "He's not the–"

"What authority do you have?" interjected the Chussman.

"I have more authority than any Zhaes bystander that you will gain in your proselytizing, Chussman. Provide me with a chance to speak with him and you will be compensated for your cooperation." She revealed the coinage in her personal bag.

"We are not mercenaries." said the Chussman.

Aerhee showed a confident smile. "I did not suggest you were."

"It can't hurt," said the Chusswoman. "We could use some extra payment."

"We were sent to gather rejectionists, not bribes," replied the Chussman.

"Maybe she can help us gather more," pleaded the Sleffman. "She must be a rejectionist."

"She said she wasn't." The Chussman turned back to her. "Are you?"

"I'm willing to provide your leaders with intrigue from the Zhaes nobility."

The Chussman turned from the circle to hear her offer. "Why would we trust the credibility of your gossip?"

"I told you before, I met that Chussman Stolk while in Fayis. He was with a Sleffman... Pur...Porth was his name."

"Captain Port!" exclaimed the young Sleffman.

"Yes, Port! That was his name. Young, anxious."

"Meeting with our captains?" said the young Sleffman. "She must be an ally!"

The Chussman held a hand up to silence his comrade. "Why were you in Fayis, let alone with our superiors?"

"The road to Kzhek is long enough for such a story," she said with a sly grin.

The Chussman chuckle. "The name is Renntik. Let's see what this story holds."

Renntik left the others to continue their work in the village while he accompanied Aerhee to Kzhek. Aerhee left the others with coins to rent ghete for their journey home, as she and Renntik took the carriage that they had arrived in back to Kzhek.

As they rode, Renntik shared some of his story as a rejectionist, seemingly hoping to gain insight into Aerhee's credibility. A Chussman from east Slinn, Renntik claimed that he joined the Allegiant three years before the Krall's assassination. Two years after the Pact of Province enforced harvesting in four of the six Courts, he was coerced by Sleffmen rebels to join their organization. Following the Allegiant's plot to assassinate the 'Chussman traitor', he left his wife and two sons in the care of his sister and her family, knowing that it was his duty to Cheric to see harvesting abolished. He spoke with such conviction and emotion that he and Aerhee shed tears twice upon the road.

She was not as willing to give full discretion of her life but admitted to being the Caser. She could not recall ever having such a positive conversation with a Chussman, let alone a mere trooper.

As promised, he delivered her safely into Kzhek, to the doors of the Krall's palace. Much of the central square and its surrounding districts were left desolate, as expected, but the restoration efforts had already begun. Scaffolding lined the sides of collapsed Canton walls as Sleffmen, Chussmen, and Tchoyasmen alike labored to repair them.

They left their ghete to be directed to the stables by young Sleff troopers on the side of the Palace. As she followed Renntik up the staircase to the main doors, she was relieved to see that he would see her inside rather than leave her to enter the Harmony Allegiant's territory on her own.

Members of the Harmony Allegiant filled the frontmost chamber dressed for all manners of occupations. A well-armored guard stood at each side of the doorway. The floor was reminiscent of a market as scribes passed through hallways as varieties of people entered and exited rooms. Aerhee had initially doubted the support for their cause, but was pleased to see how productive the city had already proven to be.

"If you are who you claim to be, *Caser*, lead the way." Renntik said.

"Don't try to attract too much attention. They might not *like* me here."

He attempted to placate her but followed her suppressed anxiety to the doors of the Krall's throne room. As expected, a guard stood at each side of the door with hand spears bound to their grips.

"Is Colrig here?" asked Renntik, earning a scowl from each guard through the slits of their helms.

"State your business?" the left guard spoke with a muffled voice. The armor proved useful in many circumstances but was a poor buffer for communication.

"I have brought him the Caser of Court Zhaes."

They relaxed as they gazed upon the Zhaeswoman.

Turning to each other, they spoke with the gargling whispers reminiscent of tumbling stones in a tunnel. "Wait here." The right guard entered the chamber while the other kept a statue's glare on Aerhee.

A minute passed before the clatter of boots echoed across the chamber to the door. A Sleffman swung the doors outward and met his guests with triumphant glee.

"Caser Kleeh!" he exclaimed. "Great catch, Chussman!"

The guards approached her with arms ready to seize her.

"No no no! Colrig this is—' Renntik waved his hands to dispel the confusion.

Aerhee stepped back despite their momentary halt. "Sir Colrig," she spoke with a worried wrinkle in her brow. *It is time to confess*, she told herself, *you are ready to change. This is only the beginning.* "I wish to advocate your cause. I want to join the Harmony Allegiant."

EPILOGUE

"Zeir?"

Footsteps approached the door and opened. "Aerhee?" Her husband stared back at her.

She ran to embrace him; her arms weakened and fell onto his slender, yet broad shoulders. "Zeir, I —"

He caressed the back of her head as he did in their early years of marriage, only stopping at her request. She had drifted like an artist's magnum opus blown in a storm, but he remained the young artist, ever chasing his prized possession.

She had been absent for weeks, forgoing any thought of sending a letter.

"You," she laughed as she wiped tears from her eyes, "are more than I could ever ask for in a companion." Wiping her eyes, she faced him with palms on his shoulders. "I mean it this time." She thought about mentioning her pledge to join the Allegiant, but now was not the time for her. It was the time for him. For them. "I want you to remember how things were when we were first courting, that's what I will become once again even if I have to defy Laeih himself to achieve it."

Zeir smirked. "Welcome back, my love."

Cracked knuckles and a parched tongue were pleasant greetings. Phenmir had arrived in Sliin.

He left for his home Court soon after restorations began in central Kzhek. It was due time that Sliin received equal attention.

He gazed out through the carriage window. Chaos following the Krall's assassination had left the city damaged, but it was nothing in comparison to Kzhek. Despite the city's wounds, it seemed at peace. He had been away long enough for the unrest to still, but there was still much to do.

The coachman had been ordered to take him into central Sliin, but he had not yet been provided with a specific destination.

Phenmir ruminated upon his most important tasks. He had to see that a new Krall was appointed, that the entirety of Court Chuss was informed of the Allegiant's progression, and that the Chussmen were ready to advocate the Allegiant's cause. *Where to begin? Who–*

"Coachman!" He opened the small window pane behind the coachman's seat.

"Yes, Thane Stolk?"

"Take me to the Canton of Endowment!"

The evening was approaching like the melt after a snowfall. Even though snow rarely fell in Chuss, even during the Zeemer season, Phenmir had a fondness for it. He exited the carriage and dismissed the coachman with a coin for gratuity.

He ran inside, pulling aside the first person he could see. "Excuse me Chussman, but are there any Endowers here at this hour?"

He shook his head with a disappointed frown. "I am afraid their mothers have all called them back to bed," laughed the laborer. He continued to walk forward with two large tomes held in his hand, but stopped with an abrupt turn. "Are you that... that one... that left to..." His eyes widened as he realized that he had ignored Phenmir's armament.

"—that left to join the forces against harvesting?"

"Yes!" He nearly dropped the topmost tome from his sweaty palms. "Indeed, you are! The Thane of Harmony!"

"How did you–does everyone know about me?" Phenmir asked, trying to speak with slight politeness to avoid sounding vain.

"You have become a hero! I heard much about you personally from a young Tchoyaswoman that has been working alongside our Endowers."

"Kaela! Is she here?" he exclaimed.

"If I had recognized you, I would have taken you to see her straight away! I only hope that she has not yet fallen asleep. Such a diligent girl for her age. Follow me, Thane Stolk."

They exited through the back doors of the Canton, approaching the Chuss Thane of Endowment's homestead on the property.

"Thane Mortiff was pleased to have her as a guest and was more than willing to offer her a room in his own residence. He and his wife do not have children, as you likely know, and were delighted to host her." He guided Phenmir to the door and knocked twice.

The door swung open. "Phenmir?" asked Thane Mortriff. "I thought you were in Fayis?"

"Much more has occurred since our time in Fayis. I have just arrived from... we can discuss this in the morning. Is Kaela here?"

"She should rest now," the Thane grinned, "but it will be a pleasant surprise for her to see one of her heroes again." He opened the door to lead Phenmir inside, dismissing the laborer with a thankful wave.

Phenmir was relieved to see that the grime from traveling had fallen off on the dry streets of Sliin, not wishing to tarnish the beauty of Thane Mortriff's well-kempt residence.

He led Phenmir to the top floor, each of them stepping past the Thane's wife, who had fallen asleep reading from *The Tome of Charity* beside a crackling fire. They approached the first door in the left hallway, sweat perspiring in Phenmir's palms as he rubbed his fingers together. The Thane knocked on the door and stepped back to allow Phenmir to stand nearest to the entrance.

"Coming." Joy filled Phenmir's soul as he heard the familiar voice of a young girl. The door opened a mere moment later and a serval mask stared at Phenmir. Despite the barrier, he recognized the glee in her countenance. She rushed to hug his legs.

"It's great to see you, Kaela."

"I did it, Thane Stolk!"

"You did what?" he asked.

"I've united the Chuss Endowers! Well, with Thane Mortriff's help."

"She did most of the work," said the Thane. "I helped gather them, not too difficult a task for the Thane that oversees them, and she followed what she had practiced in Court Tchoyas. There is still plenty of work to do, but we have a sure start."

"Wonderful," He chuckled.

"Where are the others?" She broke away from the embrace.

"In Kzhek."

"In Kzhek?" she was astonished that they had advanced without her. "Did we win? Is Zhaes ours?"

He noted that Thane Mortriff was struck with similar astonishment. "Yes, in a way, but there is much more to discuss. It's late. We can talk in the morning."

"You aren't my father and neither is Thane Mortriff. Tell me now."

"I suppose I am not, though I must keep it brief."

Thane Mortriff escorted them into his study chamber, where he then relayed the recent events. Kaela was ecstatic to hear about the triumph of the Gorgers and the contribution of the Endower Beastlings. Fear seeped through her reactions as he told them about the kaesan, which Thane Mortriff was skeptical to believe.

"I cannot wait to show Voln the army that I've built!" Her excitement dwindled into a yawn.

"We'll leave the planning for later. You need some rest and your Endowers need you in your best contention."

She nodded as they returned to her room, bidding farewell with the Tchoyas salute.

"Do you need a ghete or a place to sleep for the night, Phenmir?" asked Thane Mortriff. "It is quite late for traveling."

"I do not live far from here. Thank you for the offer, but I think my wife would like a late surprise."

The carriage rattled across a stony trail with violent bumps. A large stone in the path woke Yetrik as his resting head hit the side of the carriage wall.

He wiped his eyes and found that the sun had just started to rise. Royss and Runith remained asleep while the Endowers spoke to each other in whispers as they stared and pointed at the passing landscape.

His back ached from sleeping against the carriage wall. Royss sat across from him with no sign of apparent discomfort, only causing discomfort to the others with voluminous snoring. Seeing the Thane of Agriculture, he recalled the events in Fayis prior to their departure.

The Caser fled from the scene before Thane Trhet had concluded his justification for murder. Yetrik would have joined her if Royss had not persuaded him otherwise. No other member of their party was opposed to the act, but only Royss exclaimed gratitude to the Krall for his actions, as if he had expected it.

Witnessing their deaths would become a lifelong trauma. Yetrik remained calm, but later fell into a state of panic in conversation with Royss.

"This is *war*, Yetrik." he told him

Royss comforted Yetrik, eventually aiding him to view the situation with a sound mind. The act was not admirable, but necessary. The Thane had grown to become his mentor in a world of clouded morality. Royss taught him that the line between right and wrong was an obscure cloud that drifted to each side of the scale. On occasion, a grim decision must be favored for the triumph of righteousness.

Royss' caution returned to him. "Against all, Shaera and Blenn shall *never* know the truth of what has occurred. They will learn that it was an attack from outside forces, or something of the likes, the details will be fixed by Krall Trhet. We need them placated and compliant for our journey to the south."

As Yetrik turned to the Endowers, they both moved to press their faces to the window.

"Tree people!" shouted Blenn with the tongues on his mask pressed against the widow.

"No, that is what children call them. My mother calls them crop people," retorted Shaera.

"*We* are children! But–"

"Middlemen is the proper name," said Royss, awakened by their exclamations. "Crop people is the term used in Bard's tales."

Yetrik was lost to wonderment as he pressed himself between the Endowers. "Stop the carriage. We've found them!"

Royss opened the small window latch and informed the coachmen to halt their progression.

"They've noticed us," Yetrik told Royss.

Royss called for the Endower to return to their seats. "Blenn, have you had any visions about our interactions with them?"

"The young leaf clings unto the branch."

"What?" Royss scowled.

"The young leaf clings unto the branch," repeated Blenn. "Those words have been stuck in my head ever since we started on the bumpy road."

"Any vision?"

"No, just words. For Foretellers, it's usually words or a picture, only sometimes we see a vision."

Royss nodded, retaining his scowl of confusion. "We will all step out, but stay back with Yetrik while Shaera and Runith approach them." He turned to Shaera. "Do what you need to do, but let Runith lead."

"What do they sound like?" she asked. "How am I supposed to mimic their speech?"

"Try talking to them and listen. I don't care. That is for you and Runith to find out. Yetrik and I will stand back and observe. Are we all prepared?"

The party exchanged glances and looked back at Royss with a mutual nod.

Runith was the first to exit, placing his boots on the field of reeds, reminiscent of verdant wheat. Two middlemen stood fifty paces out from the carriage, each one holding what looked like a basket of harvested goods.

As Runith and Shaera neared the alien beings, Yetrik recognized the term "Crop people" was not far from the truth. Their bodies were the shape of a human, but were made of a conglomeration of twisted vines. The only variation from their pattern was their faces, pale and smooth skin of marble, like a masterpiece sculpture, and eyes with an astonishing yellow glow.

Runith held Shaera's hand as he approached the most proximal of the couple.

"Heloath," he said, watching for any reaction.

Shaera took a deep breath in and let it out in a harmonious pattern. *Sniff puff puff sniff puff sniff puff.*

Sniff puff puff sniff puff sniff puff, repeated the middleman.

"What in Laeih's name was that?" Runith asked Shaera in a harsh whisper.

"He spoke with his breath, so I did the same thing!"

"You understand it?"

"Yes, you try!"

"How?" asked Yetrik.

Shaera shrugged. "I don't know, it just feels natural, like talking to you. We talk with words, they talk with breaths."

Runith hyperventilated, lacking the characteristic pattern that Shaera had breathed with, to no avail. The middleman stared at him in silence. "I don't get it."

Sniff puff puff sniff puff sniff puff.

Runith turned behind him to see that Blenn was approaching them with the same pattern of respirations, Yetrik close at his side.

Puff sniff sniff sniff puff sniff puff! The Middleman seemed exhilarated by the second Endower's response. It lowered its basket and began to approach the Endowers.

"Stand back!" Royss shouted as he approached them. The Middleman took no note of his warning.

"No, Royss, they want to talk!" Shaera and Blenn approached the Middleman.

The Endowers spoke with the Middleman and were soon joined by the second with a symphony of respiration patterns.

"*The young leaf clings unto the branch,*" Yetrik quoted Blenn's prophecy.

"What?" Royss asked, turning his attention to the Yetrik

"The young! The young are the Endowers and the branch is the middlemen!"

Royss gave no hint that he understood.

"Beastlings cannot communicate with them, it is the Endowers! Middlemen can speak with Endowers!"

Yetrik took in the actuality before him as the legends of his childhood were manifest. Shaera and Blenn would provide adequate diplomats for the initial peace offerings, but were the abilities of the Endowed truly obsolete in Middlemen communication?

It seemed that the mystery of the Endower births had some connection to the Middlemen. Only the Endowers could speak and understand the language of breathing patterns.

The Middlemen were the key to unraveling it all.

AFTERWORD

Thank you for taking your time to read this book! As an independent author, your opinion of this book can make a big difference. Please take a few moments to review this book on Goodreads, Amazon, and anywhere else you would like to. If you enjoyed reading this, please tell your friends and family about it! Thank you for taking your time to read Elegy, a Duet will come soon...

ACKNOWLEDGEMENTS

I had to battle over whom I would choose to take the throne of my dedication page. Myka, you won. Once again, this book would never be here without you. The other contender was my greatest supporter, my artist that listened to endless ramblings over my dreams. Look at it now, we did it. This expression is for my wife, Sima, the first one to read my book and to actually think it was worth something. I love you. I cannot go without thanking my parents, who raised me to read and encouraged all of my dreams. You two made this dream a reality over twenty-four years of nurturing.

Though I doubt he will ever read this, another "this book would never be here without you" goes out to the lord of fantasy, Brandon Sanderson. After Myka's Dungeons and Dragons stories inspired me to write, I turned to my favorite author's wonderful lecture series on YouTube. Everything that I learned about writing fantasy began in his enlightening lectures. Thank you, sir.

After I started writing, I turned to a trusted friend and mentor from my teenage years, Steven Heumann, who is also an outstanding author. He was the first indie author that I turned to, providing me with a realistic base once I finished my first draft. From there, I made one of the best decisions of my life: reaching out to an indie author. Kian Ardalan, author of *The Eleventh Cycle*, not only provided me with some initial resources, but he sat down to talk with me for a good hour about the writing world. Kian helped me recognize that indie publishing was the way for me to go.

Once I entered the indie community, I was able to work with some amazing authors who provided me with such useful guidance. Michael Michel helped me all throughout the process with reliable information from his success with *The Price of Power*. Once I learned about the beauty of independent literature, I quickly found myself reading Zamil Akhtar's *Gunmetal Gods* series. Zamil provided me with the first professional feedback on my first chapter. Thank you, friend.

As I dove deeper into indie fantasy, I quickly found the highly acclaimed *Threadlight* trilogy by Zack Argyle, who has served as my indie author father. That was only the beginning. After I completed my second draft, I submitted my first chapter to the Indie Fantasy Fund contest, run by Zack and his wife, Bookborn (one of my favorite booktubers). I was beyond blessed to win one of their awards to receive a full editing service from Sarah Chorn. If you know anything about independent fiction, you know that Sarah is the King and Queen maker of fantasy legends. If I did not have Sarah helping with this book, it would be worse than rotting ghete flesh. Thank you Sarah, you made my dream come to life. I cannot go forward without thanking the Pendragon's workshop, my first writing group that helped me shape this novel in its early days. You know who you are. Thank you all for helping shape this book.

Along my way, I was able to receive some great help from some other amazing traditional authors like Gourav Mohanty and Ken Liu. Thank you two for the advice and encouragement to continue writing my dreams.

I must thank God more than anyone else. My faith and the knowledge obtained throughout my life helped me make this journey a spiritual one, as much as it is physical. I've felt God guide me through this process and testify that his hand has shaped me more than anyone ever could have.

412 ELEGY OF A FRAGMENTED VINEYARD

The list of people I could thank is endless. I continue to receive help along the way and cannot thank all of you enough. Everyone who has read this book or taken a chance on this fantasy freak's dream, I thank you.

I love you all more than you know and can't wait for you all to read what else is in store. Big things are coming. Thanks for joining my journey.

With love,

Kaden Love

ABOUT THE AUTHOR

Kaden Love wrote his debut novel in his final year of nursing school. Dedicated to his craft, he is ready to begin an epoch of unique fantasy. Inspired by the works of George R. R. Martin, Brandon Sanderson, and Pierce Brown, he wanted to create his own worlds. He currently lives with his wife in Salt Lake City, Utah where he juggles running to audiobooks, writing, reading, and living out his own adventures.

@kadenloveauthor on Instagram, X (Twitter), and TikTok

Printed in the USA
CPSIA information can be obtained
at www.ICGtesting.com
LVHW041508230324
775296LV00002B/24